Nikki spoke in hushed tones. "You know, Carole, nothing has to happen. Now or ever. I would never do anything to hurt you. You're the one who has to decide."

"I've already decided. I wouldn't be here if I hadn't." She paused and wished it were next year. "Is it always this awkward?"

Nikki laughed. "This is fun."

"Maybe for you. I feel like I'm going to die."

Nikki laughed again and this time Carole joined her. Then, as Carole reached for her glass, Nikki took her hand and pulled her toward her. Carole went easily, without resistance, taking refuge in Nikki's shoulder, her head resting on Nikki's soft breasts. Once there, she sighed deeply and thought: Finally.

Her heart thudding, she pressed her head deeply into Nikki's plush white sweater. No bra lay beneath. She heard Nikki's heart pulse in a slow, even cadence. She inhaled her fragrance.

Nikki stroked Carole's neck. Carole's body yearned for more. She sat up and turned to Nikki. With both hands she took Nikki's face and gazed into the tranquil blue of her eyes. She drew Nikki closer.

Carole's lips moved to the blue and then hesitatingly moved toward Nikki's full inviting mouth. It was Nikki who guided Carole's head so that their lips would meet. . . .

HIGH CONTRAST

HIGH CONTRAST

By
Jessie Lattimore

NAIAD PRESS
1988

Printed in the United States of America
First Edition

Edited by Katherine V. Forrest
Cover design by Pat Tong and Bonnie Liss
    (Phoenix Graphics)
Typesetting by Sandi Stancil

Library of Congress Cataloging-in-Publication Data

Lattimore, Jessie.
    High contrast.

    I. Title.
PS3562.A777H54 1988   813'.54   87-31273
ISBN 0-941483-17-7

To Brandy Wilde
Whose life inspired this novel
And whose love fuels my life

WITH LOVE AND GRATITUDE

To the gifted members of El Carmen Café's Third Street Writers: Gerald Citrin, Montserrat Fontes, Katherine V. Forrest, Janet Gregory, Jeffrey N. McMahan, Karen Sandler, Naomi Sloan — for their relentless pursuit in demanding more and their haunting phrase, "You can do better." A toast to the summer of 1980 when our lives crossed.

To the proprietors of *The Algonquin of the West* — El Carmen Café — Paulino Fontes and Tony Fly, artists who, in the tradition of Mama Chonita, founder of El Carmen, opened the doors of their establishment to those who act, dance, sing, paint, write. El Carmen was a refuge for politically exiled Mexican artists during the 1930s and maintains that same spirit today nurturing the interpreters of this generation.

A special thanks to Rosa Soberanes, whose tact and kindness made our evenings a working pleasure.

To Norine Dresser, friend, teacher, fellow-writer, pilot and navigator without whose radar this novel would have remained an idea.

To Katherine V. Forrest, writer, coach, conscience and editor *par excellence.* You're a tough cookie. Thank God.

ABOUT THE AUTHOR

Jessie Lattimore has taught journalism and literature for nineteen years. She holds her M.A. in Comparative Literature. She is a member of the Screen Writers Guild West. Jessie considers traveling with her lover of fourteen years and writing two of the three greatest pleasures in life.

CONTACT PRINT I

Waco, Texas — 1960

Her dancers knew little about Ruth Randall except that, according to her, she had had only one man in her life — Stiles.
Stiles had been an ambitious pimp who didn't obey the pimping rules. People tried warning him to control himself but it was no use. Soon after he became a club bartender, he was pimping for a string of full-time hookers

1

and had eight strippers working as B-girls for him. Then suddenly he was dead — found with a peacock feather stuffed up his ass and a pink leotard wrapped around his throat.

Ruth was his woman. He never made her work after hours. No customer ever took her home. Stiles made sure that when Ruth was on stage, all she had to offer stayed on stage.

"Never let a sucker take home what he came in just to look at," he always told her.

And she never did. And when Stiles was killed, she left the stripping circuit in the East and came back home to Texas, not to strip, but to train and furnish strippers for the East, West, and Midwest.

The sun was almost down when Ruth, a brassy blonde in her fifties, drove her white 1960 Buick up to the ranch house, honked and got out. Inside the car were the five dancers she was providing for the Jaycees that night. Ruth was hot and tired. In broken Spanish she asked the servants for the owner of the ranch. Before they could answer he appeared.

"Miss Randall?" He reached out and warmly shook her hand. "Duke McCoy here.'

"Call me Ruth," she said. "I need a place for my girls to rest before they perform. I got a real baby with me — just turned eighteen — don't want her to get sick in this heat."

She herded the women out of the car. "Get settled girls, while I go check the stage and equipment."

Duke led them into the house and apologetically pointed out the dressing room facilities: one large bedroom with an adjoining bathroom. Ruth shook her head in disapproval. She returned to the car, unlocked the trunk,

2

and had the help carry the dancers' luggage to the dressing room.

Having seen the girls safely into their quarters, she turned to Duke. "Now, let's see the stage, lights, and speakers."

"We don't exactly have a stage," Duke stammered. "But we do have the best lights and speakers available. Why don't I get you a drink and we'll walk over there."

"Why don't you get me a drink **after** *I see what you got for us? I have a feeling I'll need it."*

He led her to a cow pasture, to a flatbed truck flanked by rows of benches. Attached to the back of the truck was a red, white, and blue satin banner with a glittered message, WELCOME WACO JAYCEES. Proudly, he pointed to the equipment.

He showed; silently, she judged. The speakers were satisfactory, the lights had to be re-positioned. But the truck was an insult. It was too late for changes, she conceded. Had she known it would be like this, she never would have consented to bring her girls for the arranged price.

By the time she finished appraising his facilities, she made it clearly and sarcastically known that he had gotten a bargain because never before had her dancers worked in such hick surroundings. She accepted a shot of bourbon and returned to her girls.

"Well," she said cheerfully, "it's a little rustic, but it'll do. We've seen worse places, eh Kathy?" She looked at the peeling paint on the ceiling and then smiled helplessly at her.

Kathy blew a stream of smoke out of her nose and giggled. "I'll say. This is a palace compared to McAllen, and nothing could be worse than that dental fraternity stag in Dallas."

3

Ruth Randall laughed, remembering some of their past one night stands. In her prime, twenty-five years ago, as she so frequently reminded her girls, she had been a headliner in Chicago, Baltimore, East St. Louis, and Calumet City. Nowadays, she was a fair, protective theatrical agent who took care of her girls.

Word about her had spread quickly, so quickly that soon former strippers of hers started referring beginners to Ruth. They came from everywhere, from all parts of the country. They were young, pretty, rather hungry, very hungry, or starved. For whatever reason, they came to Texas which was big, anonymous, open, and, if the girls came to Ruth, it was safe. No questions were asked. All they needed was a birth certificate and there were plenty of places to get that.

The way the story was told, Ruth would teach you how to strip, help you with your music and costumes, break you in — first in small clubs and at stag parties, and after she taught you all she could, she'd send you on your way to Cleveland or Chicago where she had plenty of connections. And if things didn't work out, you could always come back. "I'll always have a spot for you."

Congressmen, city officials, businessmen, could rely on Ruth to provide them with the best looking girls available in Texas. But both customers and girls had to abide by Ruth's rules: "Gents, handle them only with your eyes. Ladies, no customers allowed to handle your merchandise."

Still, there were those who would occasionally elude her watchfulness to turn a quick trick. As a precaution, Ruth always liked to mix experienced with inexperienced girls in the hope that novice strippers would be so dependent on the older dancers that the younger ones would take up all their time.

4

* * * * *

Ruth stood in the room and eyed her resting girls. They're tired, she mused, but they'll be ready to go on in an hour. She looked at the youngest of the troupe: Nikki Tauber, a 110 pound eighteen year old redhead, fast asleep with an Agatha Christie novel lying on her chest. She was to make her stripping debut that night. Some debut. A flatbed truck in the middle of a cow pasture.

She had first seen this girl barely twenty-four hours ago and now Ruth knew that she had become a major stepping stone in this girl's life.

Janice, Nikki's lover, had brought Nikki to Ruth. A former stripper, Janice was Ruth's all-time favorite girl. No one could compare with Janice. Her sleepy green eyes, her Louisiana drawl, her slow deliberate cat-like walk kept her in demand. But she had quit the circuit to manage her new girlfriend.

Nikki's name had been changed immediately to Brandy Wilde to go with her waist-length red hair. Ruth had been struck by Nikki's fragile, cherub-like beauty.

"She's sure pretty, but is she tough enough to take goin' on the road?" she had bluntly asked Janice, in Nikki's presence.

Janice answered, "Why not? That red hair, that white skin, those blue-blue eyes ought to go over real big in the Lone Star state. Red, white, and blue, get it? Hell, Ruth, they might make her their new flag. Besides," she added, "Nikki's thought about this long and hard. It's what she wants to do — for now, at least."

Janice put her arm around Nikki's shoulders and drew her close. She assured Ruth that Nikki could take the six day journey from Houston to Waco to Corpus Christi to Hobbs, New Mexico, and then back to Houston.

5

Ruth decided to trust Janice. The two of them threw together a wardrobe for the stripper-to-be: a pearlized long sequined gown two sizes too big, a second-hand bra, and a white sheer panel. Next they gave Nikki instructions on how to move across the stage — "An exaggerated bride's walk," Ruth told her, and to hold the center of the stage, "You bump and grind."

With determination and without complaint Nikki practiced her dance steps over and over in Ruth's office.

"That's all you'll need for where we're goin', sweetheart," Ruth promised. "Now, be back in an hour with your toothbrush and without Janice," she ordered.

This took Janice and Nikki by surprise. Despite their protests, Ruth convinced them it was a take it or leave it proposition. "You brought her this far, Janice. From now on it's her show. You know I'll take good care of her," Ruth promised. So far she had.

Driving her big Buick on the desert highway, Ruth had placed Nikki in the front seat right next to her and sang, "I Picked a Pansy from the Garden of Love," while the other four girls slept. Ruth sang Sophie Tucker songs to keep herself awake and to keep the frightened Nikki entertained. In the late afternoon, the redhead relaxed enough to doze for a little while. Finally, they reached their first stop.

Ruth walked over and affectionately prodded the girls awake. "Time to get ready. You'll be on first, Lovey."

"I'm not going to be Lovey James tonight," said a small brunette.

"Oh? Who will you be then?" asked Ruth.

"Well, I want something more classy — to go with my new gown." She held up a silver tasseled sheath. "I think Sterling Hills would go good with this."

"Oh, that's nice," said Ruth. "Don't you think so, girls?"

"Yes, that's nice," they chorused.

"Well, then I want to change my name too," piped in Sally.

"See what you started?" said Ruth to the former Lovey James.

"I want to change from Reddy Love to Reddy Whip," pouted Sally.

"That sounds silly," Kathy said.

"Stick to Reddy Love," said Ruth with finality.

Defeated, the girl agreed. "But just for tonight."

"All right, so this is the line-up. Sterling Hills, Reddy Love, Brandy Wilde, Houston Train, and we'll close with Angel Black. You hear me Kathy? We're closing with you tonight. That way you can help Nikki if there's anything she needs."

She walked over to Nikki and asked softly, "Any questions?"

"No," Nikki whispered.

"Nervous?"

"A little."

"You aren't too scared to take your clothes off, are you?"

She smiled widely. "Oh, no. That'll be the fun part."

Ruth asked, "Is that why you want to be a strip? You like to take your clothes off?"

Quickly, Nikki retorted, "I've never stripped before. But I like to be admired. Someday I'll be an actress."

Ruth rolled her eyes, then kissed Nikki on the forehead. "That's someday. Right now, be a good stripper. Okay?"

Nikki asked, "What if they won't like me?"

"Look sweetheart, men are kinda simple about what they like. You got a nice pair on top and a nice pair on the bottom, and a pretty little face. I'll suggest one thing — that you put away your little girl look and smile. **Big**. Let me see you smile again."

Nikki attempted a broad smile.

"Wet your lips a little," coached Ruth. "Now, that's better. Wider, wider. Perfect."

"I feel like my face is going to crack."

"That's just because you've been looking scared so long."

"I wish you'd let Janice come with us."

"Janice has been through it before, and nobody helped her. The only way you'll get back to her is by getting out on that stage. Right, girls?"

"Right," they echoed.

"It's always hard the first time," said Lovey, giving Nikki a quick hug.

"See?" said Ruth. "Just remember — smile. And never let that smile leave your face. One more thing, it's a stag, so the clothes come off by the end of the first trailer."

"I'll remember," answered Nikki.

Ruth gave the girls a final check, escorted them through the darkness to the gaily decorated corral, then to the pasture and the waiting truck. The lighted yard was filled with men drinking and eating. They cheered, whistled as the dancers strutted by.

"Hi ya honey!"

"I'll take the blonde one."

"Gimme the redhead."

8

"Hell, I'll take whatever's left over. They all look good."

The girls waved back but kept walking behind Ruth. She ushered Nikki, Kathy, and Houston into the cab of the truck and wished them good luck. The first girl stood by a step ladder leading to the truckbed, waiting for Ruth's cue.

"Good evening, gents," Ruth shouted.

"Evening," they shouted back.

"We've got a special show tonight for all you young bucks."

They responded with hoots and shouts.

"Fact is, we could only do this show in front of young bucks like you because the girls we have are so fresh and lovely we wouldn't want to waste them on the older boys who might have trouble standing up under their heat. You fellas look like you can take it so get ready to smolder 'cause here comes our first dancer, Miss Sterling Hills!"

Screams and whistles erupted as Sterling climbed the ladder, finally revealing herself in the lights.

In the cab of the truck Nikki listened with obvious fear as the first, second, then third songs began and ended. She turned to Kathy and blurted frantically, "She's almost done . . . I think I'm going to be sick."

"No, you're not," said Kathy. "Ruth said to give you a swig of this." She pulled out a small flask and showed it to the younger girl.

"What is it?"

"Bourbon."

"I don't drink. I'll throw up."

"That's okay. It'll keep you warm while you're up there. By the time it's ready to come up, your act will be over."

The second girl went on stage and Kathy walked a reluctant Nikki to the ladder. In silence the girls watched

9

Reddy Love's three numbers. Wild applause and howls filled the pasture as Reddy climbed down from the truck totally nude.

Ruth waited for the crowd to quiet. "This next little gal's got everything you want and more than you can handle. Give a big Texas hello to a little girl from Hollywood, Miss Brandy Wilde."

"That's you, honey. Have a swallow," Kathy said, handing Nikki the flask.

Nikki gulped it down and shuddered as the liquid burned her throat. "God help me," she murmured as she climbed the steps and onto the truck.

She shielded her eyes against the bright lights. The audience whistled and waved. She stood smiling, fidgeting until the music began.

Finally, "Blues in the Night" blared from the speakers and she moved stiffly forward. Step, side-together, pause; step, side-together, pause, she counted to herself. Smile, smile, together, side-step together. Oh, hell, where am I? I've got to get this dress off. Pause, step, side-together, pause, smile.

"Come up closer," someone bellowed. "We ain't gonna bite ya."

"She's scared."

She inched forward.

"That's better."

Gracefully, she moved her arm back and lowered the hidden zipper Janice and Ruth had sewn in for her. The dress fell heavily to the floor and Nikki stepped out if it and kicked it aside.

"That's the way, honey."

Next she unhooked her bra and threw it over the dress. "Oh yeah!"

10

When the song was almost over, Nikki unsnapped her panel.

"Look, a true redhead!"

She burped; the bourbon tasted bitter. She moved closer. As "Body and Soul" began, she started her newly learned bump and grind routine. The repetitious movements seemed to help her gain control over herself, the stage, the audience. Reacting to their cheers, she dipped and turned. By the time "Tequila" started, she felt comfortable for the first time.

It's all so simple, she said to herself, the more naked I become, the safer I am.

CONTACT PRINT II

Portland, Oregon, 1968

The sanctuary at Congregation Beth Sholem was filled with three hundred friends, relatives and business associates of Mr. and Mrs. Alan Wolston. All eyes were turned to the tall, thin, pale thirteen year old who stood proudly next to Rabbi Moskowitz at the altar.

"This morning Carole will read the Torah portion dealing with Joshua in Jericho," announced the Rabbi.

Knees trembling, the young girl cleared her dry throat and began to chant, reading in Hebrew from the scrolls rolled out before her. Three lines down, Carole's voice faltered. Confused, she lost her place. The Rabbi rescued her and she regained control.

Carole's bat mitzvah was the culmination of months of intensive preparation. Her parents had labored to help her achieve this moment — transporting her back and forth to the temple for her Hebrew lessons, helping her write her speech, arranging for the caterer and the band.

Wearing a dusty rose skirt and blouse with a white lace collar, she fought to keep herself upright in her two and a half inch high heels. Beads of sweat dotted her face. Nevertheless, her body swayed gently in rhythm to her own chanting, and when her voice gathered strength as she neared the end of her portion, a feeling of superiority washed over her. Finished, Carole helped the Rabbi roll up the scrolls; she stepped aside as her father helped the Rabbi return them to the Ark.

At the luncheon following the religious service, Carole sat at the table with her friends instead of with her parents and grandparents.

Aunt Helen came rushing over to her. "Carole, I didn't get a chance to tell you before, but you were absolutely terrific. Here's a little something for your college fund." She handed the girl a small envelope.

Carole hugged and kissed her. "Oh, Aunt Helen, thank you so much." She whispered in the older woman's ear, "I like your new hair color. Is that just for me, too?"

Aunt Helen laughed. "You're so naughty."

Carole took the envelope over to her father who stuffed it into his inside jacket pocket. She patted the bulge on his chest. "Am I rich yet, Daddy?"

"We're gettin' there." He gave her a big hug, and the roving photographer's flash captured the moment.

Her mother joined the group. "Take another one of us together," she told the photographer.

"Thank you for this wonderful day, Daddy," Carole said. "And especially for my camera and things."

Her mother said, "Let's hope you don't get bored and abandon them like you did the guitar and skis."

"That's not going to happen," her father said. "She loves photography."

Grandpa Tuchman approached and hugged Carole. "Look at this girl of ours. Like my mother used to say to my sister Sadie, 'When there are two people next to you, you're like a rose between two thorns.' "

CHAPTER ONE

Los Angeles, California — 1972

Nikki Tauber stretched full length across the bed. The alarm sounded at six-thirty and she banged it off before five seconds had elapsed. She brushed back her long red hair, a tangled mass of curls, and threw back the covers.

She walked to a full-length mirror near her bed and checked the contours of her naked body. The stomach was flat, buttocks tight; she checked no further. Over the wash basin she pinned her hair back then carefully washed off the heavily-run mascara, rouge and lipstick from the previous night. She worked around her eyes, patting carefully, not too hard, then up to the hairline with deft, soft, well-rehearsed strokes.

Face and mouth laundered, she brushed back the shoulder length red curls then carefully put her hands through her hair to affect a wind-blown look. A bit of eyebrow pencil and she was ready.

She pulled on a pair of blue pants as some would gloves. Once fitted, she wiggled around in them, checked herself in the mirror once more, then put on a top, threw a Robert Heinlein paperback in her purse, and walked down to her car. Twenty minutes had passed.

By seven a.m. she was on the Santa Monica Freeway to Cal State L.A. At seven forty-five she was having coffee; at eight she was in her usual front row seat arranging her notebook and reading the previous days' notes. When linguistics professor Dr. Simon Wynitski entered at eight-fifteen, she had been ready for five minutes.

Carole Wolston trailed in thirty minutes late. Loose leaf pieces of paper threatened to fall out of her notebook. Her red Afghani shoulder bag was tangled with her Nikon camera; together the straps posed a formidable alliance that tugged unmercifully at her neck.

Wynitski waited for her to take her usual seat next to Nikki, who automatically handed her the notes she had missed. While Nikki carefully untangled Carole's purse from her camera, Carole scribbled hurriedly. Her disheveled dark wavy hair hid her pretty face; heavy lashes shrouded her eyes. A long thin nose balanced the fullness of her mouth.

For the next hour and a half, Carole wrote everything the professor said. Nikki listened and jotted down one-third. Last minute directives poured from Wynitski's mouth and then he abruptly left the room.

In the hall, Carole asked Nikki, "Do you understand what Wynitski wants?"

"Sure do. Do you want to work on the project with me? He said we could work in teams."

Carole was surprised. "Definitely. What'll we do?" Her attention drifted; her eyes were scanning the crowded hallways.

Nikki followed Carole's line of vision.

He was medium height, with dark brown hair, and had an auburn beard not quite concealing acne-pitted skin. He wore faded jeans and a stressed leather jacket and carried a pocket book, *The Portable Hemingway*, thickened by numerous paper clips. He was professor John Parrish, English Department *wunderkind*, age twenty-six.

Carole waved and when he acknowledged her, she shifted her attention back to Nikki. She spoke hurriedly, "Listen, Nikki, I want to work with you on the project. Can we meet tomorrow — here at the library? I do want to talk with you, but I have to meet John now."

"I'm here from ten to eleven."

"Fine. We'll meet then."

"Hello, ladies," said John.

Carole leaned playfully against him. "John and Nikki, meet each other," she said.

There was a strained moment as John sought to lock glances with Nikki.

Coolly, Nikki said, "Nice meeting you, John. See you tomorrow, Carole." She walked away with slow metered precision.

John's eyes followed her rhythmic hip action until she was lost in the crowd.

Carole poked him in the ribs. "She's out of your league, hot shot. Besides, she's not your type. I am."

He looked down at her and smiled, touched her thick dark hair and pressed against her tall slender body. "You're right."

CHAPTER TWO

Carole's apartment was in Silverlake, a place she contended was the only artist's community in Los Angeles. Although bordered by Neutra, Schindler, and Lautner designed homes, it was also veined with rundown one and two bedroom apartments that accepted dogs, cats, and kids, and it was peopled with artisans and students who affectionately termed their area "The Other End" of Sunset, or "The Swish Alps." For Carole, this was the place where Renaissance people roamed. They had their

19

local sandalmaker and candlemakers. They wove, tie-dyed, batiked, and grew their own dope.

The physical features of the area matched the human montage. Hills of unexpected heights rose from the middle of a flat city, and because hill dwellers are unique, the cliffs were inhabited by residents dedicated to Balkan singing, belly dancing, mandolin orchestras, balalaika bands, a Chinese drum and bugle corps. Foxes, rabbits, raccoons, possums and skunks also shared the real estate.

Her apartment was on Roselin Place, which was on top of India, one of the city's highest hills. She had a panoramic view of both the Golden State Freeway and the forest of pine trees surrounding the tiny silver lake. She loved her view because the trees reminded her of Portland, Oregon, where she was born and where her family had become a successful part of Pacific Northwest commerce as a result of the foresight of her great-grandmother, Chana, after whom Carole was named.

According to her father, Carole's artistic ability came from this mythical ancestor who had supported the family by designing sturdy woolen workpants for lumbermen. From that simple beginning, Forest Mills Clothing had grown and after three generations had become an institution in the Northwest.

Inspired by her great-grandmother's achievements, Carole left Oregon, not because there was anything wrong with Oregon, but because she was the first female offspring in the family and felt compelled to prove herself in unknown waters. She chose Los Angeles because New York was too big.

Her parents had seen to it that Carole's every wish was fulfilled with the best that her father's clothing and mail order business could afford. However, in Los Angeles she chose to live on a set allowance and in a racially-mixed neighborhood so that she could be "near real people," an experience denied her in Oregon where economic classes and religious boundaries were clearly drawn and adhered to.

John stood looking at one wall of her living room which was covered with black and white stills, all printed by her. "They're mesmerizing," he said. "No matter how much I look at your work, I always find something new."

"Look above the bed," Carole said.

He saw a large poster of Senator George McGovern with a caption that read, "The most urgent moral priority in America today is to end the curse of racism and all its ugly forms." Around the poster was a new series of black and white face shots. "Where do you find these people?"

"Sunset Boulevard, Hollywood Boulevard, Echo Park, Watts."

"Watts? When did you go down there? Are you crazy?"

"Oh, John, don't start. Besides, I was working on this before I met you. But we never got around to talking much in the beginning."

"How long have we been meeting like this?" he teased.

"Six months. Do your class souvenirs usually last this long?"

"I gotta admit, you hold the record."

She pushed him onto the bed and collapsed over him, letting her hair cover his face. "You bastard." She reached down and unsnapped his jeans. "Grow," she growled playfully.

She fondled him into an erection and together they experienced comfortable lovemaking, the kind shared by those who delve into their mates and draw pleasure selfishly for themselves but with mutual consent.

She finished first and he followed almost immediately and burst out in loud laughter and relief with his last thrust. "Who said intellectuals can't fuck?"

His comment jarred her sense of completeness. She slapped his behind as he lay over her.

She tried to steady her breath. "Who said you were an intellectual?"

She wiggled to free herself from his weight and he clamped his legs over hers like a vise.

"What's the matter?"

"Nothing," she answered, straining to keep her voice casual, yet determined to be free of him. Annoyed, she pounded his shoulders and he rolled off her.

She rose slowly and he held out a hand to her. "Are you okay?" he asked.

"I just wasn't ready to start talking yet."

"Carole, don't romanticize fucking."

"Save those comments for your classroom. They're bound to hook some new candidates." She picked up her clothes from the floor and dressed.

"Jesus, Carole, what's happening? Ten minutes ago we were having a good time."

"Can we talk about something else?" She handed him his clothes. "What did you think of Nikki?"

"You mean the redhead?"

"You phony. Your eyes were popping out. Not that I blame you. Working with her is going to save my ass in that class."

"Is the chick smart, too?"

She sat on the bed next to him and gave him a poke in the stomach. "You mean besides beautiful? Yeah, she's smart — a bit too grade conscious. The teacher's crazy about her and not exactly nuts about me. She's going into library science."

John sat up. "What a waste of tits."

"She's really nice and different. I would've dropped the class if not for her. Usually sexy types like that aren't friendly to other females."

John chuckled. "I think it's usually the other way around." He got dressed. "I've gotta get back to campus."

Listening to him, Carole's agitation subsided and she remembered that although she had started her sex life at seventeen, it was not until she was twenty-two and slept with John that she had experienced the words, "come," "climax," "over the top," "orgasm."

Since then she had used the words to describe all that excited her. An emerging print in the dark room, a creased face in the streets, a piece of music, would always be heralded by Carole's pronouncement, "Look at that. My God, I'm coming," or "I'm going to cli-max right now." The first time she made love with John she had yelled, "It's an orgasm!" so loudly that he had pulled out and looked behind him.

With the mutual understanding that they were not in love, they had stayed together because of a sexual interest of longer duration than either had ever known. It was perhaps due to this mutual understanding that occasionally they related to each other the fears and dreams that possessed them.

To her he had admitted one night, a night when wine and early morning love permitted no dishonesty, "I'm drying out — incapable of a literary erection. Since I can't sire ideas, I seduce students."

To him she could confess her desire to be a Diane Arbus, and had even expressed sadness that the Vietnam War was ending before she graduated. She was now

23

betting on the Middle East. She saw herself as the photo-journalist who would be able to shrink the size of the planet with a single shot. She seriously believed that someday if she traveled far enough she would find the face, the occasion, that would, in a single picture, disclose to the world that the fate of one was the fate of all.

All this and more they had disclosed to each other and they treasured the honesty of their disclosures.

Before leaving, he again surveyed the wall behind the bed and grunted approval of her new collection of portraits. He stared at a photograph of two winos playing cards sitting on orange crates with the federal housing projects in the background.

"They're good, Carole, though no card will ever change that one's destiny," he said, pointing to a dissipated, time-worn face.

Protective, she touched the black man on her wall. "Fuck off, John."

He kissed her lightly and walked out. She felt compelled to again touch the picture of the card player; she didn't. John's comment had soured her feeling for it.

Journal Entry — October 28, 1972

He did it again — the bastard. I don't know why I let him do this to me. I don't understand him. There's something self-destructive about him. He deliberately pushes me away — no real intimacy can start. Like a puppy, I keep running back. I feel controlled.

I hate the way he leers at every pretty girl. I don't trust him. He flirts with anyone, even in front of me. He did it yesterday — with Nikki. I'm glad she ignored him.

To be honest — I'm using him too — for sex.

CHAPTER THREE

Carole found Nikki waiting for her in the library. "Sorry I'm late," she said breathlessly. "I was up printing till two a.m."

Playfully Nikki chucked Carole under the chin. "No excuses. Let's get to work. I have it all mapped out."

While Nikki meticulously outlined the proposed research paper, the photographer in Carole appraised the scene before her.

She saw a beautiful woman with red curly hair worn loosely around her shoulders, with porcelain skin dotted by a few light freckles, with large, wide-set blue eyes and a small full mouth. Nikki wore a turquoise long sleeved corduroy pants suit. On her right hand were three gold rings, each a distinctive piece of jewelry but paradoxically, all three united to form a singularly decorative ensemble. On her left hand she wore a solitary peridot, its green shade complementing her pants suit.

"I tell you Carole," Nikki said, "nobody's ever done a dictionary of striptease terminology before."

Carole wrinkled her nose in disapproval. "I can see why. Who'd want to?"

Nikki held up her hand in protest. "Stop, before you embarrass yourself and say something you'll regret. I've been a stripper for twelve years."

"You're kidding." Carole uttered. She heard the derisive tone in her own voice.

"Yes," Nikki answered simply.

"You're really a stripper? I thought you might be a model. I mean you do look like an eight by ten glossy."

"I work at the Crystal Palace, every night except Sunday."

"Every night?" exclaimed Carole thinking of their eight o'clock class three times a week and that Nikki was always perfectly dressed. "I never met a stripper before. You don't look like one."

She faltered into silence. She looked more closely at Nikki and studied every feature — the delicate upturned nose, the softness of the contours of her cheeks, the way they seemed to flow down into the two hollows beneath. Nikki's eyes followed Carole's gaze as it moved slowly across her face; then, almost imperceptibly, Nikki raised her chin as if to give the younger woman the best possible perspective. Nikki held her pose and Carole enjoyed what she saw.

Nikki broke the spell. "After twelve years of stripping, I know the jargon. What I don't have is the time to work with it. So I'll give you the words and definitions and you put it together. I figure Wynitski would like it. What do you think?"

Carole had failed to tune in. Nikki's long, silent stare finally forced her back to business. She nodded approval and stared back at Nikki who sat with her hands neatly folded, peridot on top.

How, Carole wondered, could a person with Nikki's looks *just be a stripper?* She fought her scorn for Nikki's work. It must pay well, she thought, looking at Nikki's rings. She said, "How come you never stopped? Why didn't you try something else?"

Nikki snapped, "Because I like it. Stripping's been very good to me." She added, "I've done commercials, movie bits, but I prefer the live audience." Her voice softened. "I'm under no illusions. I know this is a bail-out profession. I'm milking it as long as I can."

Unprepared for such openness, Carole fumbled for another topic. "You never married?"

Nikki shook her head, then laughed. "Oh, I get it. Vital statistics time. I'm thirty years old — born in Long Beach. I've stripped everywhere from Texas to Paris to Singapore to Tel Aviv. No children, no husband, no boyfriend. When I get my degree I'm going to retire from the circuit and switch to daytime life. My fantasy is to be surrounded by books in peace and quiet. After twelve years I've earned it." Nikki threw out her chest. "Oh, and I'm Jewish. Does that make me more acceptable?"

Astonished, Carole raised her eyebrows in disbelief. "I never heard of a Jewish stripper. I'm Jewish, too, but not

27

enough, according to my parents." Feeling naive, she was compelled to supply spicy details of her life. "I'm twenty-two and having my first real affair now. It's with John. You met him. Nothing permanent — just my first good sexual relationship. I want as much experience from life as possible. I think it'll help my work. Know what I mean?"

Carole rambled on, becoming aware of Nikki's obvious disinterest. This puzzled as well as pained her. In the past Nikki had always seemed amused by her, but now she showed no curiosity for these most personal details of her life.

"I'm boring you, aren't I?"

Nikki smiled, reached over and gently cupped Carole's hands. "That's not it, honey. It's just that chatting is not what we came here to do. We'll book another time for socializing."

As Nikki methodically gathered her notes, carefully stacking the papers so that all corners matched, Carole felt dismissed. She watched Nikki walk away. Turn around one more time, she ordered mentally. But the redhead did not. Carole looked at her hands and felt Nikki's warmth still on them.

She thought of Nikki's jeweled hands and spread hers out before her. No jewelry, no fingernails to speak of, just plain strong working hands.

Carole left the library and strolled over to John's office in the English Department. As she arrived at his door, she heard the laughter of women's voices.

"Hello dear," Carole said casually as she breezed in. "I just dropped the kids off at nursery school. I'll pick up your shirts on the way home. Anything else you want me to do?" She pecked John lightly on the cheek and glanced at the girls. "Hello."

"Very funny, Carole." He turned to the girls, "We'll talk later."

"Bye Dr. Parrish," said a small thin blonde. Her dark haired companion smiled broadly at him.

"So, Mrs. Parrish, what can I do for you? That was a cute little trick."

"I thought so. I hope I spoiled things for you. Which one is it? The blonde or the brunette?"

"You didn't spoil anything for me. The Promotions Committee already did that. My job's on the line. I haven't published in over a year."

"I'm sorry, John." Carole hugged him. "I came up to share some good news. Remember that project Nikki and I were going to work on? It's a striptease dictionary — all her idea. Guess what she does for a living?"

"Let me see, don't tell me." He spoke in a monotone. "One, she's a stripper. Two, she's a stripper. Three, she strips."

"Why are you being sarcastic? Anyway, would you think she could be a stripper?"

"She's got a good ass."

"What about mine?" She wriggled and placed his hand on her behind. She felt no response from him. "John, am I plain?"

"You mean, compared to her? She's beautiful, but flashy. You have a different kind of beauty — more natural. I like it."

"I wouldn't be caught dead stripping."

"I thought you liked her."

She grimaced. "I do like her, but if she's so smart, and she is, how come she's a stripper?"

"Your middle class is showing."

29

"I think strippers must be exhibitionists who get off that way — especially her, doing it for twelve years. You should see the jewelry she has . . ."

"Maybe she hooks on the side. So tell me about this dictionary."

"It's never been done before. We think Wynitski will really go for it."

"I could help you guys get it published. I'll even pay you for it. I need my name on something, fast."

Carole balked at his encroachment. "Well, I don't know. Let me talk to Nikki. It's really her idea."

"Hell, I'll talk to her. When are you seeing her?"

Again she felt threatened. "Tomorrow, but you better let me do it. She's not that easy to deal with. But, I promise I'll ask."

Carole and Nikki had been working in the library for five hours and were now in the P section of the dictionary. They moved from "parade" to "pasties."

"Are they really custom-made for the dancer?" asked Carole. "Who makes them? I never heard of a pasty-maker."

"Most dancers make their own. You have to. Not all nipples are the same size."

Carole burst out laughing. "I never really thought about it."

"Well, they aren't," continued Nikki seriously. "I worked with a little girl from Paraguay, a teenie, tiny little girl and her's were the size of a nickel."

"A nickel? I wonder what size coin mine are?" She put her index finger over her blouse and tried tracing the size of her nipple. "A little bigger than a quarter."

30

Nikki laughed. "I also worked with a girl with some this big." She made a large circle with both index fingers and her thumbs.

"Like saucers? Yecch. Can you make pasties?"

"Sure. I make them for myself and other strips all the time."

"Oh, terrific." Carole slapped her hands excitedly. "Show me how. I want to surprise John."

"After we hand in the paper."

"Speaking of John, I've been telling him all about our paper and he said he'd like to help us get it published. If he can put his name on it, he'll pay us. You know how brilliant he is. He wrote a book, and . . ."

Nikki glared at her. Carole felt doors slamming shut.

Emphasizing every word, Nikki said,"I had no idea our conversations were monitored." She hesitated only briefly, then announced, "Let's each do our own paper." Rapidly she gathered her materials and walked away.

Shocked, Carole chased after her. She called desperately, "Wait for me. We'll forget John. Let's just do it." She walked alongside Nikki.

"Let John help you, Carole."

"He can't even help himself. He's in a bind."

Nikki stopped, turned, and placed her hand firmly on Carole's shoulder. "It would never work. There's still time for you to do a paper of your own."

"What about all the work I've put in already?" she asked angrily. "I've done all the typing. And that damned bibliography wasn't easy. I've already put in ten hours of hard work, Nikki."

"That guy's a leach and he's using you. And you're using me." Nikki walked away.

31

CHAPTER FOUR

Journal Entry — November 5, 1972

I've been dishonest. Under the guise of friendship I agreed to work with Nikki on a paper whose topic I thought was beneath me. I've changed my mind. What's more, after spending those hours with her, I feel a rare sense of respect and admiration for that beautiful woman. Hers is a quiet strength. There's something scary about it.

I feel guilty. I let John use me. I was willing to betray her to please him. If he's a shit, so am I. I owe Nikki an apology. I have to find her before I lose my nerve. Besides, she's got to take me back on the project.

For two days Carole tried calling Nikki. No one answered. She tried going to the usual places on campus to find her, without success.

After Nikki failed to show for two of Wynitski's classes, Carole decided to go to the Crystal Palace. She took all her spare cash, forty-seven dollars and fifty cents. Unsure about what to wear she chose a long black skirt, a black turtleneck sweater which showed off her brightly colored African trade beads. She applied heavy makeup.

A wave of depression closed over her as she drove to the Crystal Palace, a place that by its very name was the antithesis of the cozy green surroundings she had known while growing up and what she had created for herself in her first own apartment. She thought of her darkroom, her records, the possessions that brought security into her life.

A dark man dressed in red and black livery opened her car door. "Good evening. Welcome to the Crystal Palace." Startled, she mumbled something and walked toward the pulsating bulbs of the marquee. She looked for a hint of Nikki's name among Alberta Pacino, Torchy Allen, Brandy Wilde, Precious Pearl, Dreamy Daniels, Lotus Linn.

At the front door a large imposing woman checked her ID, collected five dollars and waved her in. The interior was very dark. A waitress in a silver sequined costume offered to seat her near the stage, but Carole shook her head and went to a table at the back. She leaned back,

33

affecting an I've-been-here-before pose and ordered a rum and coke. But she knew she revealed her ignorance when she tried to pull her nailed-down chair closer to the table. She waited a while, then checked the chairs around her. They too were bolted down.

"We don't want the customers rearranging things, honey," the grinning waitress explained.

Between acts the music blared loudly the heavy beat of a Tom Jones song. Carole's attention was drawn to the shiny, cold, but lavish decor. The club was only half full of patrons. Two couples sat together, the women looking bored but their husbands obviously delighted by the heavy breasted waitresses who deliberately rubbed against them while serving drinks. At other tables, expressionless men sat alone, dressed in everything from work khakis to executive garb. She was fascinated by a group of expensively tailored Japanese men who sat in silence, patiently awaiting the next act.

"Ladies and Gentlemen, the Crystal Palace is proud to present poetry in motion with Miss Torchy Allan."

To the opening bars of "Tropical Heat Wave," and extravagantly dressed brunette shimmied onstage to the accompaniment of polite, scattered handclapping.

Several college boys sitting ringside whispered to each other and laughed loudly at the dancer. She glanced provocatively at them and then selected the quiet one among them as her target. She played to him licking her thumb, slowly inserting it in and out of her mouth. He squirmed as his buddies jeered.

Could this be the live audience Nikki prefers? Carole wondered.

She saw four attractively dressed women quietly absorbed in the show. Why were *they* here? She turned

34

her head away from the now-nude performer who was licking a long icicle lollipop while sitting astride a chair.

A husky voice asked, "Are you ready for another, Hon?" The waitress' hips pressed against Carole.

Startled, she murmured, "Yes."

With the opening bars of "Temptation" the dancer fell to her knees. Using a lavender fur rug, the woman, knees apart, touched and caressed her body slowly, invitingly, sensuously. In slow motion she crawled to the edge of the stage. This time she focused on the most raucous member of the college group. She silenced him by lifting and lowering her pelvis while staring directly at him with lips opening and closing in anticipation of climax.

The audience howled, especially the victim's buddies. Satisfied with her retaliation, the dancer leaned forward, and with her finger, planted a kiss on his nose. She stood, took a bow, tossed her hair back with one hand and walked offstage without looking back. Cheered by the audience, she reappeared and took another bow.

"And now for your pleasure, the Crystal Palace looks East to bring you our very own Precious Pearl of the Orient, the former Miss Nude Tokyo."

Carole winced as she tried to match the Chinese strains of "Fan Tan Fanny" with the Japanese trappings of kimono, obi, gata, and parasol. Pearl did little other than open and shut her parasol as the music switched to a shortened version of "Un Bel Di Vedremo."

Feeling restless, Carole finished her second drink and asked the hovering waitress, "When is Nikki coming on?"

"Who?"

"Nikki, you know . . . red hair, with the curls?"

"You mean Brandy. She follows Pearl."

"Would you tell her something for me?"

"Write it down."

Carole scribbled on a napkin, I'M HERE. PLEASE TALK TO ME. CAROLE (FROM SCHOOL).

Carole suffered through the rest of the pseudo Japanese performance, understanding the tepid response of the Japanese tourists in the audience. Nikki is next, she thought. I hope she's good.

The emcee carried an antique clothes pole onstage. *"And now ladies and gentlemen, the epitome of seductive femininity, Miss Brandy Wilde."*

Applause was sporadic as "Mademoiselle de Paree" came over the loudspeaker. At first Carole failed to recognize Nikki in a long, tight-fitting, turn-of-the-century black dress. Her eyes and mouth were vividly accentuated; her hair was tucked beneath a black silk turban. She stood at the back of the stage and waited several bars before beginning her dance.

Nikki moved with subtlety — swaying her hips gently and beckoning an unseen lover to her. Her steps were slow, deliberate, full of innuendo, as if promising a certain someone an intimate night of love.

Carole was relieved that she could watch without embarrassment. She's magnificent, she thought, moments later. Carole was surprised that she enjoyed watching, and then was shocked to discover that she was the only one still clapping as the first song ended and Nikki removed her gown.

More French songs followed. As Aznavour sang "Old Fashioned Way," Nikki, clad in a sheer negligee, went into her finale. She used the peignoir with artistry, covering one part of her body as another was revealed, teasing playfully, coyly, and then finally dropping the silken cover, allowing her audience the complete view.

Carole watched enthralled, as Nikki teased, smiled, and narcissistically caressed herself.

The audience responded with enthusiasm. Taking advantage of the crowd's involvement, Carole waved at Nikki who appeared to be looking directly at her. No response. Feeling rejected, Carole wondered if Nikki had even seen her. She looked for the waitress to ask if the note had been delivered. With a pang of guilt she remembered scoffing at Nikki for being a stripper; she reddened at the memory of that conversation with John.

She felt a light tap on her shoulder; it was Nikki clad in a black evening gown — nothing underneath. "Did you enjoy the show?"

"I was afraid you wouldn't come."

"May I sit down?" asked Nikki.

"Please. I want you to know I'm sorry. I've been looking for you lately. You haven't been at school. That's not like you."

"I've been working on my new act."

"I like the one you just did. You're so much better than —" Carole checked herself.

"So what brings you here?"

"Nikki, I was stupid. I never wanted to include John. He talked me into it. Let me do the paper with you. I've put in a lot of time already."

"It's true, you've done your share of the work," Nikki conceded. "I was furious because he was trying to steal my work. I know you like him but I don't want him near me."

"He's really not bad. It's the publishing trap he's in."

Carole saw Nikki's anger resurfacing and quickly added, "I didn't come here to talk about him. I came to admit I was wrong." Carole felt a lump in her throat; then tears started.

Nikki reached over and gently pushed the hair away from Carole's eyes. "Hey, it's okay. You've made your point. Besides, I'm also pressed for time."

With the rush of relief came a new onslaught of tears. Nikki passed Carole a cocktail napkin to wipe her runny nose. "You're a wonderful dancer, Nikki," she said, sniffling.

"I have to go now," Nikki said. "Let's meet tomorrow at my place and get caught up."

As Nikki rose, Carole did too. She signaled for the check. Nikki disappeared as suddenly as she had arrived. Carole looked at the bill, six thirty-six. Feeling generous she dropped eight dollars on the tray and left.

"She's in. I'm out, huh?"

"I'm sorry, John," said Carole. "That's the only way she'll do it. I have my own needs."

"You know what, you stupid bitch?" His grin taunted. "I was thinking about your needs too — your photography career."

"Tell me again where you think you could get our term paper published?" asked Carole sarcastically.

"*Language in Society* is a possibility. They've published articles with photographs before. That's where you come in. You've never shown before."

Carole laughed. "T and A pictures in a scholarly journal? You must really think I'm stupid."

John ran his fingers through his hair. "All right. I'll write two versions. One for academia and another for *Cosmo* or *Playboy*. You can still do your paper with Nikki. She'll never know the difference."

"John, I'll know the difference," Carole protested. "I can't do that to her."

"It could land you a job," he said.

"And give yours a shot of adrenaline, too," said Carole tiredly.

He glared at her.

CHAPTER FIVE

High rent district, Carole thought as she tracked down Nikki's address on Holmby Avenue in Los Angeles. Maybe she has a rich boyfriend.

Opening the door, Nikki said, "Coffee's ready."

Carole stepped into a spacious airy apartment. "Nice place."

"I'll give you a tour later. Let's get started. Everything's on the kitchen table."

Carole followed Nikki down a hall whose walls were lined with photographs of Nikki and other dancers. "Neat pictures. Who took them? The lighting is —"

Nikki took her by the hand and pulled her toward the kitchen. "I'll tell you the whole story later."

They worked until mid-afternoon when the doorbell sounded. "Oh, shit, is it that late?" Nikki said, getting up. "My friends are here to help me with my new act. It opens this week."

Carole heard Nikki explain at the door, "We're still working."

A hard-edged voice commented, "So your new little friend is still here?"

Carole felt a pang of discomfort. She stood as Nikki ushered her friends into the kitchen.

"Lorayne and Alice, this is Carole."

Lorayne's darkness captured Carole's eye immediately. Complexion, hair, eyes — even her glance was dark. A beautiful woman, Carole thought and about my age. With tightly crossed arms, Lorayne leaned against the wall glaring at her.

Frightened by such hostility, Carole shifted her attention to Alice, an attractive, small-framed woman in her thirties. Expensively attired in a Patinos pants suit, she had that same packaged look as Nikki did. Everything went together, from her coiffure to her matching purse and shoes.

An uncomfortable silence followed the introductions. Nikki turned to her friends. "Wait for me in the living room. Fix yourselves a drink."

Carole could see Nikki's nervousness. "Do you want me to leave? I could come back later."

"Screw it. Why don't you stay while I rehearse, and when I'm done we'll finish the paper. Wait here while I tell them."

Carole could hear muffled explanations and apologies. Nikki returned and asked her to wait in the living room while she put on her costume.

Avoiding Lorayne, Carole sat next to Alice.

Alice smiled. "Are you studying the same thing Nikki is?"

"No, I'm in photo-journalism. Are you dancers, too?"

Lorayne looked away.

Alice answered, "I stripped with Nikki years ago at the Largo." She lit a cigarette and after an exaggerated inhale proclaimed, "Now I'm a courtesan."

Carole chuckled politely, then realized that Alice was not trying to be funny. "A courtesan? I don't understand."

Alice dragged some more on her cigarette, crossed her legs, leaned back on the cushions, then winked impishly at Carole. "I'm an ex-hooker and an ex-stripper, and now I'm the mistress of a very wealthy man."

Carole laughed to herself. If I had never met Nikki, I would have gone through my entire life without meeting a stripper-hooker-courtesan.

"I love shocking people," Alice said, grinning. She continued, "I'm paid to keep him happy, go wherever he goes, and look pretty. I even shave my legs twice a day, something I learned from that course for women on how to be alluring."

Carole frowned, showing her distaste. "I read about that seminar. Divine Femininity. It sounded terrible. It makes slaves out of women."

42

"This well-paid slave ain't complaining." Alice displayed a heavily jeweled hand.

Nikki called from the other room, "Start the cassette."

Alice turned on the cassette player; an instrumental rendition of "My Funny Valentine" began. Nikki came out of the bedroom wearing a long white eyelet gown trimmed at the hem with small red felt hearts. She cradled a heart-shaped box.

Throughout the rehearsal Nikki and Alice agreed or disagreed over which was the most graceful way of removing the bloomers, the smoothest way of disposing of the box, the quickest manner of unhooking the corselette. The music was stopped continually, reversed, sped forward. Carole was relieved when Nikki announced, "Let's do it again, but this time without any interruptions."

Enthralled, Carole watched Nikki. She wore no makeup; there were no lighting effects to heighten the drama, no men to play to; yet she was as compelling to watch as she had been the first time. Her steps were smooth, sensual, her body movements rhythmical, flowing.

She cast seductive glances at Alice, then Lorayne. Carole waited in anticipation for her turn. When it came, she flushed; warmth coursed through her body. And she returned Nikki's gaze. Finding the central depth of Nikki's eyes, she stayed with her, fighting every impulse to look away. Nikki smiled knowingly at her and released her.

Nikki was now in the final stages of disrobing and Carole's eyes followed her hands as she caressed her arms, breasts, thighs. She was luxuriously celebrating herself and Carole vicariously participated in the ritual. Her breathing became shallow and heat pulsed rapidly through her.

Something's happening to me. She brushed aside the alarm and gave her eyes permission to explore Nikki's body.

A uniform creamy color, Nikki's skin was satiny smoothness interrupted only by a light spray of freckles across her shoulders, and a small strawberry mark on her right breast. The pale pink nipples stood erect as she brushed her hands gently across her full firm breasts. Carole stared at the reddish triangle of curly hair below the tiny waist. Long muscular legs accentuated the shapeliness of her round hips.

Something forced Carole to turn her head. Lorayne was staring at her with an angry accusing look. Self-conscious and confused, Carole looked away and gave her attention back to Nikki. The magic was gone. For the remainder of the dance, Carole could only feel Lorayne's eyes upon her. She had become this woman's prey.

The dance ended and Alice and Carole applauded. Nikki bowed, graciously accepting their enthusiasm. Still naked, dewy with perspiration, she sat on the couch on the other side of Alice. Amused, Carole watched them: one dressed to the teeth and the other completely naked except for high heels.

Turning to Lorayne, Nikki asked, "Honey, would you fix me a drink? Carole, would you like something?"

"Nothing, thanks." Carole could too clearly imagine Lorayne flinging a highball glass at her.

"Now," said Nikki to Alice, "tell me the truth. Do you think it's too long?"

"I'd test it for a week before making any changes," Alice recommended. "If you go on the road this summer, you'll need all fifteen minutes."

Lorayne brought a drink, then hurried to the bedroom and returned with a robe. She laid it dramatically over Nikki's knees, and glowered at Carole as if to say, *Show's over.* Nikki accepted the robe, apparently oblivious to the tension between Carole and Lorayne.

Carol waited for a break in the conversation before voicing what she had silently rehearsed. "Nikki, you said we'd get back to work after you finished."

Alice took the cue. "Come on Lorayne. Let's go so the schoolgirls can do their work."

Lorayne answered, "I want to talk to Nikki for a minute — alone."

Once they were out of the room Carole turned to Alice. "That girl hates me. I don't even know her."

"She's just moody," Alice said with a shrug, her gaze sliding away from Carole.

"She's glared at me all afternoon."

Alice chuckled. She stretched, getting ready to leave. "Let it go, honey."

Nikki walked her friends to the door. Once alone with Nikki, Carole said, "I liked Alice, but your other friend . . . I thought Lorayne was going to hit me."

"Lorayne is kind of funny sometimes," Nikki agreed. "But she's a fine actress — a little eccentric. Now let's finish the damned paper."

They worked until early evening. Nikki used the three-hole punch on the finished paper. "Now Carole," she teased, "don't sneak John a xerox of this."

Carole giggled. "I haven't seen him. He's mad at me. Maybe I should call him."

"Let him call you."

45

"I'm not proud. If I want somebody I'll chase him anywhere . . . work, home, wherever."

"You can get hurt that way," Nikki warned. "Do you really want him?"

"I don't know. I've gotten used to him. How about you? Is there someone special in your life? You've never mentioned anyone."

"I'm seeing someone now."

Carole sat up in her chair. "Tell me about him."

"Not much to tell."

"Do you love him?"

"Carole, you're so nosy," Nikki chided softly.

"Okay, forget it. I get the hint. I don't love John, but he's been the only excitement in my life." Remembering the thrill that Nikki had stirred in her during the dance, she blushed, and added hurriedly, "It's getting late."

"Carole, I'm glad we sorted things out." Nikki reached over and gently placed a hand on Carole's arm. "I'm not working weekends anymore. Maybe we can get together."

Carole put her hand over Nikki's. "Good. I don't want to lose you again. Thanks for letting me watch you rehearse. Between that and striptease jargon I'm beginning to feel like a real expert."

Nikki laughed. "Oh yeah? Maybe I'll teach you how."

Thrilled by the idea, Carole shrieked, "Would you, really?"

"If you really want to, I will. Don't tell me you're overcoming your prejudices."

Embarrassed, Carole stammered, "I was such an ass. I'm sorry."

"You're not alone. Lots of women feel that way. I'll call you to set a date for your first lesson." Nikki walked her to the door and hugged her goodbye.

Elated, Carole ran down the stairs as Lorayne was coming up. They exchanged glances and Carole laughed impulsively, calling out, "Fun seeing you again, Lorayne."

CONTACT PRINT III

Cleveland, Ohio — 1963

Driving a 1953 yellow Ford convertible, Janice drove to the front of the Plaza Hotel where Curly put up all of his out-of-town dancers. She honked several times, but the shabbily uniformed doorman ignored her.

"Should I get out and get him?" asked Nikki.

"Let me," said Janice. "Remember, you're a dancer."

Twelve striptease clubs and a couple of good restaurants lined Short Vincent Street. The day Janice brought Nikki to work at The Bright Spot, the local paper ran a banner headline, CHAMPAGNE FOR LOVE, as part of a continuing exposé of clubs which supposedly lured patrons into paying seventy-five dollars for a bottle of champagne. The paper specifically mentioned The Bright Spot because the owner, Curly Zakis, was called the Mayor of Short Vincent Street.

Janice walked up to the doorman, and pointed to Nikki in the convertible. "That's Curly Zakis' new dancer," she announced in her polite Southern drawl. "Are you going to tell her to bring in her own luggage?"

The doorman looked at Nikki who was in full makeup. "No, Ma'am," he answered hurriedly. He rushed to open the car door. "Welcome to the Plaza, Miss. I'll see that the luggage gets to your room."

The room was white, clean, and airy. Over the double bed hung a tropical seascape with a burnt orange setting sun. Gold brocade drapery covered an entire wall. Janice walked over to the drapes. "Don't tell me we have a view?" She pulled the drawstrings. A two-foot square window overlooked the alley behind the hotel and the delivery entrances of small shops and restaurants. She laughed. "I knew it was too good to be true."

"Forget the view," said Nikki. "We have a TV!" She switched it on. "I've read every book I packed, at least twice."

A loud hum filled the room. A frenetic, heavily-accented voice warned, "Lucy, I don't want you coming to the club tonight."

"Look Janice! Lucy!" Nikki stretched out on the bed and stared at the TV.

49

*Janice looked at her watch and lay down next to Nikki.
"You've got two hours to rest, shower, put on fresh makeup
and get to the club."*

*Nikki pulled Janice's arm around her and snuggled.
"I can rest watching TV. Just stay here with me."*

*"Of course I'll stay with you." Her hand gently stroked
Nikki's red hair. Before "I Love Lucy" ended, Nikki was in
a deep sleep. With a soundless chuckle, Janice carefully
pulled her arm away, doubled the green crushed velvet
bedspread over Nikki and kissed her on the forehead.*

*Janice stared at the sleeping Nikki. Behind all that
makeup, she could still see the child who had captured her
heart three years ago.*

*Sadness invaded her as she recalled the shock of
finding Nikki at her front door, her worldly possessions in
one suitcase and three brown paper shopping bags.*

*"Mother told me to either stop seeing you or get out,"
Nikki had said simply.*

*Janice's efforts to make Nikki reconsider her choice
had failed. Her final argument had been, "We'll always be
outsiders."*

"Not if we stay together," Nikki said firmly.

*And when her mother came clamoring and raging
after her, threatening to put Janice in jail, promising to
have her killed, Nikki was granite in her resolution.
"Mother, I love her. She didn't talk me into this — it was
the other way around. And I swear to you — if you do
anything to hurt Janice, I'll find a way to hurt myself even
more."*

*Janice looked around their hotel room, put water on to
boil on the hotplate, unpacked her tea. The sadness within
her lifted as she re-lived the abandon of Nikki's passion
when Nikki had fallen in love with her.*

She looked at Nikki wrapped up in the bedspread and wondered where she herself would be if they had never met. In unguarded moments like this, she faced the fear that the weight of Nikki's love might someday become a burden — or that Nikki's ambition might one day drive them apart.

Janice studied the sleeping Nikki. What will I do when I'm no longer enough for you?

CHAPTER SIX

Journal Entry — December 6, 1972

I'm lonely. I called John to make up. Like a fool, I believed him when he said he'd come over. The sun's gone down and I'm still waiting. I know a lot of people, but I have no one special. I am the center of no one's life. It's like I'm everywhere and nowhere. All I have is this worn our little journal to deposit my feelings.

To be honest, I never wanted to be close to anyone except John — and how much of that was sex? After so much time with Nikki, I thought perhaps we could stay friends. I feel like I could really talk to her. The intimacy I need has nothing to do with sex. I shouldn't be alone.

From the street, Carole could see the lights on in Nikki's apartment. Relieved, she hurried up the stairs and rang the doorbell several times. No answer. She knocked; after several raps, a voice called out, "Who is it?"

"Nikki, it's Carole."

Slowly the door opened. Nikki's head emerged.

Carole barged through the doorway. "I need to talk."

Nikki tied the sash on her robe. Her voice was cold, unwelcoming. "What do you want?"

"I'm so depressed. John stood me up —"

"It's late, Carole," Nikki interrupted. "I have someone here."

Carole plopped in a chair. Nikki approached her and said firmly, "You have to go home. Do you hear me? I'll call you tomorrow."

At last Carole recognized Nikki's anger. Carole's gaze drifted across the apartment to the phone off the hook and two empty highball glasses. She looked toward Nikki's bedroom and saw a figure in bed. She jumped up and moved closer to Nikki and whispered apologetically, "Why didn't you tell me you were with someone?"

Again, Carole peered into the bedroom. The person was sitting up, now. Lorayne. Mortified, Carole looked at Nikki. "Why didn't you tell me?"

"I would have, eventually."

"Like hell."

CONTACT PRINT IV

-

Suzanne and Julie.

Carole was twelve years old and away at camp for the first time. One morning she hurried back to the bunkhouse to get her camera for the nature walk. Her sneakers trod silently across the wooden floor. Camera in hand, she was startled by muffled sounds. On a bunkbed, at the far end of the cabin, two of the counselors, Suzanne and Julie, were lying together. Their tops were off; they were kissing; Suzanne had her hand inside Julie's shorts. Carole was afraid to move, afraid they might see her. A strange excitement stirred within her. Although she wanted to stay, fear of being discovered forced her to creep out. But for the remainder of her two weeks' stay, she spent every moment spying on Julie and Suzanne.

Carole sat up in bed, reached for the phone and gave the operator a Portland number. "Mom? No, I'm fine, really. I didn't wake you up, did I? I just felt like hearing your voice. How's Dad? Are you guys still depressed about McGovern losing the election? Me too. Anything new with Amy? I got an A on my linguistics project. No, there's no problem. Sorry I woke you. I didn't know it was so close to midnight. Give my love to Dad and Amy. I love you too. . . ."

Nikki finished her dance and gracefully left the stage. The next stripper stood waiting in the wings. "It's a dead house," Nikki warned.

Backstage she entered the small dressing room she shared with two other dancers. The wall was covered with clothes hooks and hangers on which hung gowns, negligees, hats, and head-pieces. Lashes, eye shadow, lip gloss, paints, brushes, wigs and feathers were strewn all over the dressing tables. She hung her clothes and slipped into a robe.

Her roommates were watching Johnny Carson on a portable TV. Nikki glanced at it uninterestedly. Restless, she joined two other strippers in another dressing room; they were working on a jigsaw puzzle. After trying to fit in a piece or two herself, Nikki returned to her own dressing room. Picking up her new textbook, she tried to read. She let the book fall.

CHAPTER SEVEN

Wearing a burgundy-colored pants suit, Nikki stood waiting by Carole's car. Her nose was buried in a copy of *Atlas Shrugged.*

Shocked to see her, Carole asked, "What the hell are you doing here?"

Nikki smiled. "I want to talk to you, but not here. Can you give me a ride home?"

"What happened to your car?"

"I don't have it today."

They rode in silence to Nikki's apartment. While Carole drove she felt Nikki looking at her. Carole's favorite pair of jeans and T-shirt suddenly felt outlandishly shabby. Why should I care how I look around her? she thought, in irritation.

"You can park over there," Nikki said as they pulled in front of her apartment house.

"I can't stay long."

"Carole, relax. I'm not going to touch you."

Carole shrugged. "I know that."

In the apartment, Carole glanced into the bedroom and saw an empty, neatly-made bed.

"No one's there," said Nikki.

"It doesn't matter," Carole said tiredly.

Nikki chuckled. "Is that why you've been avoiding me for two weeks?"

Carole sat. "I'm sorry, it's just that now I feel uncomfortable around you."

Nikki sat on the couch opposite Carole. "Because I'm a lesbian?"

Carole flinched.

"Does that revolt you? Frighten you?"

Carole looked away, avoiding Nikki's eyes. "I'm not sure."

"Why?"

"I feel threatened."

"Carole, do you think I've been trying to seduce you?"

Carole was embarrassed.

Nikki looked at her and added, "You're wrong if you think so."

Exasperated, Carole blurted, "I made such a fool of myself the other night. I just wish you'd have told me."

"Once people find out you're gay, they change toward you. You're a perfect example."

59

Carole allowed Nikki's statement to sink in. "How long have you been this way?"

Nikki sat quietly, her eyes distant. "Since I was eighteen. I met an older woman, Janice. She was an ex-stripper and gay." Nikki removed her jacket and folded it neatly beside her. "I never had feeling toward women before her. But suddenly she became the most important person in my life. And I ran away to be with her and she taught me how to strip. I liked it. I was good at it." Nikki smiled as if pleased with herself. "I got to see the world and she went with me. For eight years we traveled everywhere together."

"Eight years? Together?"

"It should have lasted longer." Nikki sighed. "We were in Singapore. She got tired of being on the road with me, came home, and that's when she met June. We're only close friends, now."

Carole thought she saw pain in Nikki's eyes. "Do you still care for her?" she asked cautiously.

Nikki shook her head vehemently. "The romance is dead, if that's what you're asking."

"Don't get mad. It's hard for me to think of women living together that long. I didn't know things could get that serious."

"Why should it be different for us than for anyone else?" Nikki spoke emphatically. "If anything, love that defies conformity winds up being stronger. It was for me, anyway."

"I never thought about it that way," Carole admitted. "I don't think I've known any gay women. At least, I couldn't tell if they were gay. You certainly don't look it."

Nikki said wryly, "We come in all shapes and sizes."

"Lorayne doesn't look gay either." Carole asked hesitantly, "Is she your main person now?"

"We see each other frequently, but lately we've been having a lot of problems and," Nikki added with a barb in her tone, "your visit the other night sure didn't help."

Remembering the evening, Carole covered her face with her hands. "Don't remind me. Do your parents know?"

"Not Dad. For some reason Mom wants to spare him. I think she hopes someday I'll meet a nice man and straighten out." Nikki chuckled.

Carole tried to imagine herself in such a situation. "My folks would die. They're so protective." She shuddered. "I haven't even told them about John. They think he's just a boyfriend. If they knew he was my teacher, they'd probably report him."

Nikki looked at her watch. "Carole, do me a favor. Drop me off to pick up my car."

"Sure. So you really didn't have a car today?"

Nikki said, "It's a new car — a beautiful green Chrysler Imperial. It's waiting for me at the dealer's."

"You're kidding. Brand new? Jesus, where do you get all your money?"

"The car's a graduation present from a friend — a male friend. And friend is all he is."

"Nikki, that's terrific!" Carole got up and hugged her. Nikki's body felt light and frail against hers. "You're so tiny. I can't believe I was afraid of you. I want to stay friends. Do you?"

"What do you think? I took three buses to get to school to meet you today."

CONTACT PRINT V

Cleveland, Ohio — 1963

    Costumes in hand, Nikki reported to Leo the bouncer at seven o'clock. The swarthy six-foot-three French-Canadian took one look at her and said, "Let's see your birth certificate."
    She set aside her clothing, reached into her purse and handed him a piece of paper.

Leo looked at her and checked the certificate. *"You're Nicole Tauber, but go by Brandy Wilde. Right?"*

Nikki nodded.

He continued. *"I'm in charge of all Curly's girls. You're never gonna have no problems. But, just in case the Beverage Control people come in, I'm gonna give you two dollars to go across the street and have dinner. Understand?"*

Nikki nodded again. "I'd like to see my dressing room, please."

"Follow me." He led her through the club which was one long room with a bar running across its length. *"Drums and sax will be on stage with you. Piano's on the side. Where're your charts?"*

Nikki smiled. "Here they are, but I've never danced to live music before. I used a jukebox in Houston."

"Big-time clubs, eh?"

"Yes," said Nikki frankly. *"My stage has been anything from restaurant aisles to plywood on top of a couple of boxes."*

Leo looked over his shoulder at her and laughed. He ushered her into the dressing room and recited by rote, *"You hang your things here. Don't touch nobody else's stuff. Don't hang your things in the middle of theirs, even if you don't know what belongs to who. I don't like to break up girl fights. Understand?"*

Nikki's eyes opened wide. "Girl fights?"

"Some of them are real scrappers. Hang up your stuff and come back to the bar. I'll buy you a Coke and show you how you can make a lot of money."

Leo was setting up the well drink bottles when Nikki joined him. She had to hop to get onto the bar stool. He laughed loudly at her. *"This is the layout, low-pockets. We* go from eight-thirty to three in the morning. You'll do four fifteen-minute shows a night."

Nikki asked, "I have an hour and a half break between shows?"

"No, you work all the time. You change after your show, then you come out and sit with the B-girls. They get a percentage of every drink customers buy them." He added eagerly, "Dancers get more."

Nikki frowned. "I really don't like mixing with the customers."

"That's the way it's done here," he said curtly. "Now, you get a five dollar commission on every bottle of champagne, and two bucks for a split. Some guys won't buy the bubbly and are gonna wanna buy you a regular drink instead. You let them know if they wanna sit with you, they gotta buy you a minimum of two drinks. But you get no commission on that."

Nikki pushed away the Coke. "That set-up isn't going to work for me. I don't drink."

"I told you I'd take care of you. Watch carefully." Leo put a double shot glass in front of her and filled it with vodka. "The bartender will put your booze in this. Then he's gonna give you a water chaser in a small glass that'll be half full."

Leo downed the vodka and immediately took a swig of the water. "See what I did?" he asked.

"You drank the vodka," said Nikki matter-of-factly.

Leo chortled loudly. "Fooled ya! I don't drink either! I spit the booze back into the chaser glass."

Nikki wrinkled her nose. "That's disgusting."

"That's business. Now, when you spit the vodka back into the chaser glass, make sure you don't have spit bubbles showing. The B-girls will teach you. They got it down pat."

64

Nikki protested, "I still don't think I can do it."

"You have to. Your salary comes outta the drinks you sell."

Leo cleared away the glasses and wiped off the counter. From each of his pants pockets he took a revolver and laid both on the bar. With the palm of his hand he moved the drums back and forth. They spun loudly, cleanly. He put the guns back in his pockets and pulled a blackjack out of his belt. He strapped it firmly to his right wrist with adhesive tape.

Nikki jumped off the stool and moved back. Her face was pale, her lower lip trembled slightly.

He looked at her and snickered. "I was a gun runner at fifteen."

Nikki moved slowly toward Leo. "L-let me practice spitting," she stammered.

Nikki had been working at the club for several weeks. One night she approached a curly-haired blond man sitting at the bar. She sat on the stool next to him. "Hello," she said softly.

The man turned to her and slowly poured his drink on her head. The liquor ran down the front of her face and trickled down her neck and back.

Nikki froze, then in almost slow motion slid off the stool. She leaned against the bar for support, her knees buckling under her. "I — I — I better dress for my show," she said to no one in particular.

She inched her way back to the dressing room, holding onto whatever she could to keep herself steady. In the dressing room, she looked at herself in the mirror. Her eyes were smudged, giving them a bruised look. Carefully, she wiped herself clean and towel-dried her hair. Methodically, she dressed for her next show.

Shugar Cane burst into the dressing room, an empty bottle of champagne in hand. "Brandy, I just sold a bottle!" Nikki stared stonily back at her. "What's the matter?" asked Shugar.

Nikki put on her silk elbow-length gloves, jerking her fingers into place. Harshly she clasped a wide rhinestone bracelet on her wrist.

She snatched Shugar's empty bottle away from her and stormed back into the club. The curly-haired man was where she had left him. She stared at him for a long moment, her chest moving up and down. To calm herself, she placed a hand over her heart.

Swinging in a wide arc, she smashed the champagne bottle against the bar and lunged at the man. Leo leaped over the bar and threw her onto its polished surface. He turned to the stunned man and proceeded to beat him over the head with the blackjack.

The man was unconscious on the floor, his matted curls covered with blood. Leo dragged him to the backroom and searched him, emptying his pockets and wallet before dumping him into the back alley.

Shattered bottle in hand, Nikki followed and watched. "I could have killed him," she whispered. Her body shook violently. Her legs caved.

Leo caught her just as her knees hit the pavement.

"Leo," she said weakly, "I wanted him to die."

CHAPTER EIGHT

Below Carole lived a bizarre couple, Laurence and Cristina, the proud owners of Elsker, the oldest living ocelot in captivity. Cristina and Laurence were also the proud parents of an eleven-month-old son, Luke. Whenever Elsker was out of the cage, Luke was put into his own separate but identical cage.

Seeking to match what she considered Nikki's exotic lifestyle, Carole had asked her neighbors if they would permit Elsker to pose with one of the Crystal Palace strippers. They readily agreed, their only stipulation being that they wanted to watch.

For weeks Carole had phoned Nikki but rarely found her in and when she was, she was either getting ready for work or busy with homework. Obsessed with spending more time with her, Carole trumped up a photo session using Nikki as a model. She fabricated a story of a magazine contest so that she could show off her talents to the older, more sophisticated woman. She wanted Nikki to find her interesting.

That morning she cleaned her apartment from top to bottom, experimented with a little bit of makeup, and decided to pin back her normally unruly hair.

"You'll love these people," Carole promised Nikki as she walked through the door. "He's a conscientious objector assigned to the zoo." Carole stomped heavily on the floor. "I'm signaling to let them know you're here."

Nikki looked around Carole's apartment. "I hope the ocelot's a pacifist too." She walked over to Carole's wall of photographs and studied them closely. "I had no idea you were so talented."

"That makes me feel good," murmured Carole. It's working, she thought excitedly, and busied herself positioning the spotlights around the room.

"And your hair, I love it that way. I can see your face now," said Nikki, peering closely at Carole.

Embarrassed by the blue eyes so near to her, Carole looked away.

A loud rap on the door startled them both. Laurence, six-foot-five, his face covered by a leonine beard, and Cristina, swathed in an Indian sari, her hair below her buttocks, came into the room. Each carried a cage. Accustomed to the sight, Carole was reminded of its strangeness by the look of amazement on Nikki's face.

Laurence shook Nikki's hand vigorously. "I'm Laurence and this is my wife, Cristina. And in the cages are Luke and Elsker." He pointed to the baby and the wildcat. "Our kids."

Nikki walked to the cage and playfully stuck her fingers through the bars. "Your son is beautiful. Does he bite?"

Laurence laughed and winked flirtatiously. "We lock him up around sexy women."

"His father could do with a little incarceration too," added Cristina sarcastically.

"She's got you there, Laurence," Carole teased.

Nikki smiled and approached the ocelot's cage. "I love cats. May I pet her?"

Cristina assured her, "There's no danger with adults, only with children. She's been declawed."

"All right you guys," Carole announced. "I'm ready." She took out a green satin sheet and covered her couch. "Nikki, you ready?"

"Sure, no problem," Nikki said lightly. "I brought this black peignoir. Will it do?"

Laurence looked at the flimsy see-through gown. "Outta sight!"

Refusing to reveal her shock at Nikki's choice of clothing, Carole merely stated, "Uh-hum."

Nikki got her purse and took out a makeup bag. Looking into a hand mirror, she applied fresh lipstick and checked her eyeliner. She touched up her nose with clear powder and turned to Carole. "I'm making sure my face has a matte finish for you." She looked in the mirror for a final inspection. "Okay?" she asked Carole.

Carole's mouth went dry. "I'm ready when you are."

Nikki walked over into the kitchen, casually kicked off her shoes, slowly removed her white silk blouse and bra.

69

Then she peeled off the rust-colored slacks and slipped into the peignoir.

Laurence and Cristina looked away from Nikki; one played with the baby while the other stroked the ocelot.

The blood drained from Carole's face. Anger surfaced. What the hell does she think she's doing? she thought. She's in my house, for Christ's sake. "Lie down on the couch here," she ordered tersely.

Nikki walked gingerly over to the green satin sheet, ran her hand over it. "Feels nice," she said, and smiled at her audience.

Carole felt the anger wash away. She doesn't mean to embarrass me, she thought. "We want a sleepy, casual effect. Fluff out your hair, Nikki. Cristina, let Elsker out."

The ocelot made a low, rumbling growl, crouched low, then darted out of the cage. He sniffed around the house while Nikki positioned herself in a reclining pose. Making deep, guttural sounds, the cat meandered toward her.

"He'll go to you, if you call him," Cristina offered.

Nikki stretched out her arms. She whispered, "Come here, Elsker. Come here, sweet boy."

As soon as Elsker climbed onto Nikki, Carole readied her camera and pressed. The whir of the motorized drive cued Nikki to begin.

Carefully, she touched the back of the animal's intricately patterned head — first with the tips of her fingers, and finally with both of her hands. Cupping Elsker's head between her hands, she murmured, "I know you like this." The cat purred loudly. "Why, Elsker, these aren't spots. They're beautiful rosettes."

Carole's eyes followed the smooth rhythm of Nikki's hands as she familiarized herself with Elsker's muscular body. She's seducing the animal, Carole thought.

"He likes his back scratched — like me," Laurence prompted.

"Shut up,"whispered Cristina.

"Don't interrupt. Let things happen," Carole ordered, moving closer to Nikki.

Nikki continued playing with Elsker. She ran her nails through his fur; the sound of the animal's purring filled the room. "Oh, yes," she said. "This is what you want." More confidently she sat up, placed Elsker on her lap, letting her thick red hair cascade over his face. He pawed at her curls, bouncing them back and forth. Obviously amused by his kittenish behavior, Nikki hugged him and kissed his forehead.

"Keep doing that. We're almost at the end," Carole said.

Nikki continued to play coyly, seductively, affectionately with the animal. Carole noticed that Nikki's movements with the cat were similar to her stripping style — subtle, polished, narcissistic.

Carole's camera stopped. "Could one of you take Elsker off Nikki?"

"I'll do it," said Laurence.

"No. I'll do it," Cristina insisted.

"Let me play with him just a little while longer," pleaded Nikki. "He feels so good."

"Here, you can play with me," offered Laurence, stroking his beard.

"Pull in your horns, Laurence," said Carole, wishing her neighbors would disappear.

On the spur of the moment, she decided to do a black and white photo session, but without the cat. "Nikki, please take off your makeup now," said Carole, pointing to the bathroom. Turning to Laurence and Cristina, she added, "Thanks so much for Elsker. I'll make some prints for you."

"Take off what?" asked Nikki, a frown spreading across her face. "I thought you only wanted me with the ocelot."

"I want to try some shots with a natural look," Carole answered, apprehensive at Nikki's unhappy expression.

"I don't want to take off my makeup," Nikki said emphatically.

"I want to focus on the contours of your face, not your coloring." Carol was irritated. "You'll look softer without makeup."

"I don't want to do it," Nikki retorted as she moved toward her clothes on the table.

Cristina cleared her throat loudly. "Luke and Elsker have to eat now. It's been nice meeting you, Mickey," she said. She put Elsker back in the cage and handed her imprisoned son to her husband. "We hope to see you again. Laurence, would you give me a hand, please?" The family of four vanished.

Carole waited until the door closed. Walking over to Nikki, she softly explained, "You'll be just as beautiful without makeup. Trust me. I want to capture the inner person in you — something I think is quite beautiful, too."

Nikki put down her blouse. "That sounds nice, Carole. Sorry I overreacted. I don't like sudden changes. Besides, I don't like to be without my makeup," she explained.

"I've seen you without makeup," Carole added hurriedly.

"When?"

"The night with Lorayne."

Nikki smiled at her and went to the bathroom. She emerged with a clean face.

"Great," said Carole. "You can get dressed if you want to. I'm just shooting your face."

Nikki took off the peignoir and briskly put on her clothes. "You know, Carole," she said, lifting an eyebrow, "you're getting away with murder. I'm not used to taking orders."

"They aren't orders. It's something you'll be glad you did," Carole guaranteed, feeling a little guilty about the scenario she had created — all so she could spend time with this woman who had invaded all her thoughts.

Nikki flashed a warning look at Carole. "Understand I'm just going along. I don't know why." She moved closer to Carole.

Flushed, Carole turned away and walked to the refrigerator. "Light a cigarette. Get comfortable. I'll get us a beer. When you're ready, start talking to me."

"About what?"

"Anything. Shock me. Entertain me. Answer my questions. Tell me about Janice. She sounds exciting. I'd like to meet her. Why did you break up with her?" Carole turned on the spots, checked her light meter and focused her lens.

"I told you before. She fell in love with another woman. Our relationship had changed already." Nikki hesitated as if distracted by Carole's constant picture-taking. She continued, "We're still good friends. I talk to her almost every day. I keep no secrets from her. We have brunch Saturday mornings."

The fact that Nikki had a confidante made Carole envious. She wished she had one. Carole moved the camera closer. "What does she do now?"

"She's the office manager at a theatrical booking agency. She started at the bottom and now she's at the top. It wasn't easy."

"Have you gotten over her yet?"

Nikki seemed annoyed. Carole photographed that, too.

"Would you stop that?" barked Nikki.

Carole disregarded her. "Which? Taking pictures or asking questions?"

"Now I'm not sure," laughed Nikki. "Yes, I got over Janice, but she's still very important to me."

"Sort of like John and me?" asked Carole.

"Don't compare us to that," Nikki said angrily. "I felt married to Janice."

Speechless, Carole put down her camera. She laughed nervously. "Sorry, that sounds strange to me."

Nikki said caustically, "From what I can see, you and John are simply having an affair — a bad one at that."

"Not true, Nikki. We have — we had — a very meaningful relationship. I admit he stood me up the other night, but he had to go before the Committee at school. And yet," Carole continued, feeling sad, "I still feel I could turn to him if I seriously needed someone."

"That's the point, Carole," Nikki argued. "It should be more than just a to-the-rescue type of thing. When you barged into my house that night, you were running from him, not to him."

Carole turned off the spotlights and sat on the couch next to Nikki. "You're touching a sore spot. I discovered the other night that even though I know a lot of people, I have no one." She felt teary.

Nikki reached over and placed her hand on Carole's shoulder. "We're friends, Carole," she soothed.

"I'm getting maudlin." Carole changed the subject. "Let's talk about you. What's happening with Lorayne?"

"We tried living together but it didn't work. I couldn't have any friends over — she'd suspect me of carrying on with them. She said I never let her see the real me."

74

"It's the Scorpio in you," Carole teased.

"Good. You feel better," Nikki said, stroking Carole's cheek. "Are we finished shooting?"

"Sure. I'll get your makeup bag for you."

"I just want to move around." Nikki got up and stretched her legs. "When will you print the pictures?"

"Maybe this weekend." Carole felt her face redden, thinking of her deceit. "I'll make copies for you."

"What's the name of the contest you're entering them in? Janice asked me, but I forgot."

A burning sensation filled Carole's body. "Nikki, I haven't been honest with you." She pulled the pins out of her hair and heedlessly let it fall around her face. She looked at Nikki and stated flatly, "There is no contest. I concocted the whole thing to get you here."

Nikki stared at her. "You what?"

"It's true. I wanted to see you and I needed something to lure you here."

Nikki planted her feet firmly apart, placed her fists on her hips. "Tell me again what you did," she ordered.

Carole blubbered tearfully, "You're always busy. You never have time to talk. I was sure you wouldn't be willing to come over here for no reason."

Nikki glared fiercely for another moment, then burst out laughing. "I would have come without that damned smelly ocelot. Tell me, did I give you a good show?"

Carole was speechless.

"Need I remind you? I was the one who rekindled our friendship after you ran away." Nikki walked back to the couch and curled up with her feet under her. "Don't look at me that way. Say something."

"What can I say? I was trying like hell to square myself with you. And you've turned it into a joke —"

Nikki interrupted, "I'm not making fun of you."

75

"Listen," Carole demanded. "I'm not sure *what* I want from you. I'm confused. The stripping and the gay stuff bothers me." She sighed deeply. "It also excites me." Exhausted from this admission, she leaned her head back on the couch.

"You're full of contradictions," said Nikki, stroking Carole's hair. "A half hour ago you went on about wanting to photograph the real me. You even asked me to take off my makeup — which I did." Nikki paused. "The truth is, you're not interested in the real me. You're interested in my labels. Stripper and lesbian."

Carole's tears flowed freely. She wiped them away with her sleeve. "I've got something else to tell you."

"Oh Jesus." Nikki threw up her hands.

"It has nothing to do with you. It's something that happened to me a long time ago. I've been thinking about it a lot since you and Lorayne." Carole's voice grew stronger. "When I was twelve, I saw two girls together — accidentally. They were my teenage counselors at camp."

Nikki closed her eyes and smiled. She drew her hand away from Carole. "You're having a terrible day. Are you sure you want to go on with this?"

"Yes. I have to," insisted Carole. "I saw them and I ran away. The truth is, I wanted to stay. Afterward, I followed them everywhere, but I never saw . . . that . . . again. I realize now it was the first time I was sexually aroused."

"What does this have to do with me?" Nikki's voice softened. "Twelve is a sexually ambivalent age. Don't read too much into it."

"You don't understand," Carole persisted. "I was really, really excited." Her voice grew louder. "When I got home from camp, I felt all this guilt — but I never regretted watching them."

"Oh, I get it." Nikki laughed. "You're having *deja vu.* You don't know whether to run away from me or stay. Is that it?"

"Maybe," said Carole quietly. "I like you very much. I don't want lies between us."

"I don't like lies, either. In the end, they're always cruel. You leveled with me, and I should do the same with you. Don't look frightened," Nikki reassured her. "But I have to ask you, are you using me to spy on the gay world?"

"Definitely not," Carole declared hotly.

"Maybe it's not conscious. I think you're interested, but don't want to leap into the water. Is that right?"

"I never thought about that before," Carole admitted.

"It's possible to look but not touch."

"What do you mean?"

"Want to go to a gay bar? I'll take you to a couple, if you want," Nikki offered.

Uncertain, Carole kept quiet.

"Look," said Nikki gently. "They're just bars with ladies in them. There's nothing to fear. I'll keep them off you."

"Promise?"

"Promise." Nikki leaned over and gently placed her lips over Carole's.

CHAPTER NINE

Journal Entry — January 16, 1973

I could look at Nikki forever. I wish I were smaller so she could hold me tightly in her arms, then I wouldn't feel so clumsy. I don't feel good looking enough for her. Is this shallow? I thought I would die when she kissed me and touched my hair. That kiss was more than friendly. Why didn't I kiss her back? Coward. I'm losing it to her.

* * * * *

Although Nikki was to pick her up at nine, Carole had been preparing all day. Never before had her appearance been so important to her. At the cosmetics counter at Bullocks Wilshire, she spent forty-three dollars on Estee Lauder products, including a book, *Improve Your Looks with Color.* Remembering that Nikki dressed in color-coordinated pants suits, she bought an oyster-colored outfit and a bright salmon long-sleeved blouse.

To pay for this, she broke a vow she had made to herself: never to use the American Express card given to her by her parents.

She remembered her father's insistence that she take it. "Listen, you never know what can happen. Do it for me," he had pleaded, "for my peace of mind."

"Dad, you don't understand my need for independence." Then she had conceded grudgingly, "If I use it, it'll have to be a dire emergency."

She bought a pair of dark beige boots with purse to match. She toyed with having her hair straightened, but dismissed the idea. She browsed through the jewelry department, but the real stuff was out of her reach and the costume jewelry was ugly.

That afternoon she gave herself a facial and experimented freely with various makeup styles: the sultry-tempestuous look, the playful all-American girl, the career woman, the mysterious cosmopolitan. Sultry-tempestuous would take best advantage of her heavy lashes and dark eyebrows, she decided. But the liquid makeup made her look too hard, and so she opted for the all-American effect created by a little bit of blush and light lipstick.

79

She had been ready for an hour by the time Nikki arrived.

"Carole, you look lovely!" Nikki exclaimed.

Trying not to move her lips, she said, "It's been a bitch trying to decide how to get ready for tonight."

"Why are you talking that way?" asked Nikki.

"I don't want to mess up my makeup. I plucked my eyebrows for the first time. My skin's still burning."

Nikki examined them closely. "You shaped them well."

"I had to use ice to get the swelling down,"she complained, happy for the compliments, but wishing to end Nikki's scrutiny.

"It was worth it," said Nikki. "You've never looked better."

"Are you saying I usually look like a slob?"

"No." Nikki took Carole's hand. "Let's go have a good time."

Carole fought the impulse to pull her hand out of Nikki's; instead, she let herself be led to the new Chrysler.

Despite its hysterically flashing sign on Melrose, the entrance to Dion's was through an unlit side street. Standing around the entrance to the club were a group of young women affecting a tomboy roguish look.

Carole looked at their corduroy pants and vests. Shit! I'm overdressed, she thought. But if I am, Nikki's even more so.

"High society's with us tonight," called out a girl with kinky blonde hair tucked beneath a leather cap.

Nikki turned toward her and blew her a kiss.

The girl pretended to catch the kiss. "Thanks, Red. I'll tell you later where I put it."

80

Everybody but Carole burst out laughing.

Inside, a women's rock band pounded as couples danced on a crowded dimly lit dance floor. Against a wall, drinks in hand, women stood talking. Others table-hopped, giggled, gossiped.

Carole and Nikki found the only empty table — near the stage, next to the speakers. The table reverberated as the singers wailed, "I got you, Babe. I got you."

Carole cupped her hands over her ears and shouted to Nikki, "Is this supposed to be romantic?"

Nikki pointed to the dance floor where two young women danced slowly and closely, oblivious to the rhythm of the music.

Carole studied the couple for a while, then pulled her attention away to the farthest corner of the club. Two drunk women kissed and pawed at each other.

Repulsed, Carole turned away and scowled at Nikki who smiled and made an I-can't-help-it gesture. In return, Carole motioned thumbs down and called loudly, "Let's go."

Outside the club they took a deep breath of smoke-free air. "Red, back so soon?" called the girl in the leather cap.

Nikki waved a friendly goodbye and hurriedly led Carole through the crowd.

"Well, you lasted all of five minutes."

"I won't apologize," Carole spat. "Those two women were gross. The club was raunchy and the music was lousy. How can you stand going there?"

Nikki laughed. "Oh, I never come here. This is one of the roughest bars in L.A. That makes us even for the ocelot. Now I'll take you to a good place."

Papa Freud's was located at the west end of Hollywood. By any standards, it was a high class bar, complete with valet parking, thick carpeting, antique mirrored walls, and color coordinated tables and upholstered chairs. The visuals of the club immediately pleased Carole. The focal point of the room was an elevated stage where a sophisticated and well-balanced band accompanied its headliner, Cretia.

From her keyboard Cretia held court. On the piano were two glasses, one a half-filled brandy goblet, the other a small glass containing a champagne chaser. Next to the glasses was a pyramid of cigarettes. At the far end of the piano, as far removed from Cretia's line of sight as possible, was a huge brandy snifter stuffed with money.

Cretia was a black, speed-thin woman, her face thickly made up, her hair pulled back into a topknot from which tumbled a long hair-piece dotted with fresh orchids. Her form-fitting silver lamé gown was made more flamboyant by glittering jewelry on her fingers, around her neck, arms, wrists, and ears.

In a husky voice she spoke intimately into the mike. "How many Geminis tonight?" She received an enthusiastic response and chuckled derisively. "Be careful, Gems, this is a heavy month for you, hard breaks, hard breakthroughs." She punctuated her patter with minor chords and keyboard runs.

Amused, Carole looked at Nikki and smiled approvingly. "She's fantastic!" Nikki led Carole to a table against one of the mirrored walls.

Carole felt comfortable at Papa Freud's. Maybe because there's men here, she thought. The dance floor didn't seem so strange with both sexes dancing, even if it was men with men and women with women. She enjoyed looking at their outfits; they seemed more like costumes than ordinary clothing. Cowboys, Indians, sailors, Mandarins. Nikki ordered a Dubonnet cocktail for herself and a rum and Coke for Carole.

Cretia, turning her attention to a black woman sitting at the piano bar asked, "Have you ever been here before?" The woman nodded and Cretia snickered, "Well then, you know what being here is all about. Are you looking for a lover? Hmmm ... we all want some love tonight."

Suddenly Cretia began to belt out, "Rollin' on the River," an apparent favorite of the crowd, which cheered and rushed toward the dance floor. Carole watched the musicians and the dancers, envious of their pleasure-filled involvement, wishing she had the courage to join in.

"Should we?" asked Nikki, motioning to the dance floor.

Carole hesitated. "I'd feel funny."

Wordlessly, Nikki got up and walked over to a girl at the bar and asked her to dance. Angry, afraid and feeling deserted, Carole spitefully avoided looking at Nikki. She turned instead toward the stage where a black male dancer with an Isaac Hayes style shaved head, dark glasses, and a bulging crotch in skin-tight pants, bumped energetically toward Cretia. A gilded mesh vest covered his hairless chest.

When the song ended Nikki returned with two women, one of them Alice, the ex-stripper turned courtesan, who Carole had met at Nikki's apartment. She was with a pretty, tomboyish girl, approximately Carole's age.

Nikki seemed elated to have run into them and urged, "Bring your drinks over to our table. Carole, you remember Alice? And this is Vicky."

"Hi, sweetheart," Alice said to Carole. "Didn't take you long, did it?"

Carole flushed while Nikki explained, "It's not what you think. Carole was just curious about gay bars."

"We all got to start somewhere," teased Alice.

Nikki asked Alice, "How come you're here? You're always with your Daddy on Saturday nights."

"He's in Chile fighting for his copper mines," cooed Alice. She nestled closer to her young companion. "I'm Vicky's date tonight."

While Alice and Nikki gossiped and laughed, Carole deliberately excluded herself from the conversation. What am I getting into? she asked herself. Seeing Nikki in her particular world made Carole realize how little she knew about this world.

Vicky leaned over and asked Carole, "Do you go to school with Nikki?"

Carole folded her arms and looked over toward the pianist. "Yes."

"Are you going to be a librarian, too?"

Carole shrugged.

"You must excuse Carole," said Nikki. "She's never been in this kind of place before and she thinks it's catching."

Carole glared at Nikki, who turned away and continued talking with Alice.

"This is only my third time here," Vicky said shyly. "It's pretty nice, don't you think?"

"Better than Dion's," answered Carole.

Vicky raised her eyebrows. "You went there? Why?"

Pointing to Nikki, Carole said, "That's where my teacher took me."

Vicky giggled, muttering something about Nikki's peculiar sense of humor, her exact words drowned out by the noisy arrival of four women who sat at a table adjacent to them. One, a tall, blonde, rose and drunkenly swayed over to Nikki. The woman looked closely at her then pulled back in mock surprise.

"Hello, Nikki," she slurred. "Who's new in your zoo?"

Nikki said dryly, "Go back and sit down Sara. You're drunk."

Sara leered at Carole and warned, "Got watch this redhead. She breaks hearts." She returned to her table.

"Who's she?" asked Carole angrily.

"A drunk lesbian, that's all," answered Nikki. "Ignore her."

"It's difficult," said Carole. "The whole table is staring at us and talking about you."

"That's a lie," screamed Sara at the woman next to her.

"I saw you, bitch," the woman shrieked back. "The minute you saw her, you went right over to her. Admit you're after her."

"You're sick," yelled Sara. "And I'm sick of your motherfucking jealousy."

The woman slammed her fists down on the table, spilling their drinks. "Goddamn you!" She reeled from the table and roughly jostled Carole as she stumbled away.

Angrily, Carole stood up. Nikki stood with her. "Are you okay?"

"No. I want to go home."

"Why don't we move?" asked Alice placatingly.

"I'm taking her home," answered Nikki.

As they gathered their purses, Sara called out, "Don't leave, Nik. We won't hurt your little girl."

The last thing Carole heard was Cretia crooning, "And for all you lovers, remember, the Sun is in Scorpio and the Moon is in Uranus."

Nikki drove to Carole's apartment in silence. Carole leaned against the car door, as far away from her as possible. Staring ahead she remained frozen even after Nikki parked the car. Nikki opened the door and gently led her out. She fished through Carole's purse for the front door key.

Carole went to bed and curled up. Nikki looked through the closet, pulled out an overcoat, and covered her.

"It's cold in here. Where's your heater?" asked Nikki.

"Against the wall," answered Carole. "Just flip the switch."

"Are you feeling better?"

Carole only looked at her.

Nikki spoke gently, "Talk to me." She sat next to Carole on the bed.

Acutely aware of Nikki's closeness, Carole reached out a hand. Nikki held it and pressed it between her palms.

"I think I had too many expectations, and everything went wrong," Carole said. A single tear rolled across her face.

"Tell me what you wanted to happen," Nikki encouraged.

"Nothing — everything, but at the same time something big and wonderful. Am I stupid? Do you know what I'm trying to say? Help me."

"I'm trying to understand. I'm confused, too." Nikki paused. "I wasn't sure if you were out to experience the gay bar scene, or if that was an excuse to be with me. I still don't know."

Carole felt her hand grow warmer and Nikki held it tighter. "I think I wanted to be with you," she stammered. "But I was pretending I was going to see the bars." She sighed deeply. "You kissed me, remember? I think that set me off."

Nikki drew up Carole's hand and kissed it gently. "I didn't mean to frighten you. I do care — a great deal. I didn't know how sensitive you are. I should have taken better care of you this evening."

Carole sat up. "I'm not a baby." She wiped away her tears and laughed shakily. She held her arms out to Nikki. "Can't you just hold me?"

Nikki moved toward Carole and embraced her fully. "You hold me," she murmured. She nestled her head against Carole's breasts.

"This isn't the way I pictured it," whispered Carole.

"Carole, do us a favor. Don't get ahead of us."

Nikki moved closer, bringing her head to rest on Carole's lap. Leaning back against the headboard, Carole carefully outlined the fine features of Nikki's face with her fingertips.

"I can't believe you're here," said Carole. She looked down at Nikki's closed eyes, bent over and kissed them lightly. "Are you asleep?" Receiving no answer, she slowly slid Nikki's head off her lap and onto the pillow.

Tiptoeing around the bed, she removed Nikki's shoes. From the closet she pulled our her warmest quilt and carefully laid it over her. She removed her new boots and climbed into bed and snuggled next to Nikki.

When Carole woke up at dawn, she was alone.

CHAPTER TEN

In the dressing room of the Crystal Palace, Torchy and Lotus delicately lifted the top from a large square cardboard box.

Lotus peered in. "Oh, Torchy," she squealed in delight. "So many pieces!" She emptied the contents onto the card table.

"I'd rather do this than mix with the customers like we had to in Boston," said Torchy, pulling up a chair.

Nikki walked into the dressing room. "Another puzzle?" she asked sharply. "Don't you two ever get bored?"

In silence, Lotus and Torchy continued spreading out the pieces.

Nikki looked at the picture on the puzzle box. "That's all you ever do, one damn puzzle after another." She took a closer look. "Progress. You've advanced from Norman Rockwell to Picasso."

"What's the matter, Nik?" Torchy asked sarcastically. "One of your girlfriends giving you a hard time?"

"She's not my girlfriend. I don't like feeling confused. Makes me bitchy," she admitted.

"We noticed," said Lotus. "Anybody we know?"

"No," said Nikki. "She came into my life out of nowhere."

"Don't keep us in suspense," urged Torchy. "Tell us about her."

At that moment Toni burst into the room in tears, her large breasts bouncing. "Someone here has been telling awful stories about me," she sobbed.

The three women crowded around. Lotus reached for some tissue and wiped Toni's mascara-stained cheeks. "Calm down, Toni," ordered Nikki. "Tell us."

"One of the waitresses," blubbered Toni. "She's been telling customers I've got silicone and it's gone down to my legs."

Torchy asked, "How do you know she's saying that?"

"During my last number some jerk yelled out, 'Your silicone's jiggling in your knees.' "

"Whose station was he at?" demanded Nikki.

"In the back — near the bathrooms, I think."

The three dancers cried in unison, "Rosa!"

Toni started to cry again. "I've been having trouble. I didn't think anyone could tell."

Nikki said, "Toni, you have very nice breasts. Maybe if you'd put a little pancake on them to match the rest of your body, they wouldn't look so shiny in the lights."

"Yes," Torchy agreed, "that's what I do."

"Can I show you what I mean?" asked Nikki, ushering Toni toward the cosmetic-covered dresser.

Working as a team, the three women distracted Toni with chatter as they repaired her makeup.

"You don't know what silicone trouble is, Toni," said Torchy. "Remember Heidi? She had silicone put in her ass and it got infected from the constant pressure."

"What a dumb thing to do," said Nikki.

Torchy continued, "You haven't heard the worst of it. Now she has to have it removed, and part of her ass is going with it." Torchy suddenly shrieked with laughter. "What's worse, she just bought a house and signed a contract to go on the road to pay the mortgage. Can't you just see the billboard in Duluth? 'Come see Heidi Highness and her half-assed act!' "

Just as abruptly, Toni renewed her crying. "I never should've had it done. You know I was a hand model on *Peyton Place*, don't you?"

"Yes, you've mentioned it a few million times," Torchy reminded her. "We've all done something in show biz."

"I needed to do something when the show went off the air. I decided to strip, only my breasts were too small."

Nikki put her arms around Toni. "That's enough." Discreetly, she asked, "You take care of yourself, don't you?"

Toni announced with a loud tearful sigh, "I don't lift heavy things, and I don't have rough sex, if that's what you mean."

"Then I promise you," Nikki said, "your silicone's not going to move anywhere. So stop worrying now."

"Unless," said Torchy, "you had it done in Mexico."

"I'm not that stupid," said Toni. "I paid twelve hundred dollars to Dr. Hauptmann in Beverly Hills, six months ago. But I got lumps now." She pointed to her breasts. "See!"

One at a time Torchy, Nikki and Lotus examined the silicone lumps on Toni's large breasts.

Lotus whistled. "Twelve hundred. That's steep. Mine was seven fifty, but that was ten years ago when it was legal."

Torchy snorted. "They don't put big tits on orientals."

Nikki laughed. "Speaking of old bust jobs, I gotta tell you this story Janice told me. In the fifties she worked with an old stripper who'd had paraffin put in her tits. Before going on stage, she'd have buckets and buckets of ice brought to her dressing room — in top secret. Then she'd freeze and shape her tits with ice packs."

"Sounds like some of Janice's old-time bull to me," scoffed Torchy.

"No, listen," insisted Nikki. "The other strips couldn't figure out what all that ice and all the hush-hush was about, so they went around the outside of the club and peeked in the window and there she was — packing them in ice. She could only do a seven minute show because the lights would soften the paraffin and her tits would hang down to her waist."

Everyone laughed but Toni. "I don't know whether to laugh or cry," she said.

Nikki tossed her a tissue. "Laugh, honey. We're tired of wiping your pretty face."

Carole insisted angrily, "I swear, John, I just went to find out what it was like."

John studied Carole's face. "What upset you?"

"Maybe when some of her friends thought she and I were a couple. That pissed me off."

"Come on, Carole. You *are* attracted to her. And she does spend time with you," he teased. "I know I got the shaft when she came in the picture."

Bluntly, Carole said, "Let's keep this honest. Our first break came when you wanted me to do something crooked with her work to save your ass at school."

"You've changed, cookie, and I think it's because of her. As long as you're mad anyway, I'm going to tell you something. I think you and Nikki have a thing going, only you're stallin' at the gate."

"I'm not stalling. I just don't think she likes me — that way."

John raised his eyebrows in surprise. "Really? You'd go through with it?"

Carole admitted, "I think so. Does that shock you?"

"Personally, I don't like it, but there's nothing wrong with it."

"Oh, sure, some of your best friends —"

John interrupted, "I didn't say that. But if you're obsessed with it, do it and get it out of your system. Look, I've considered it myself."

"You have?" asked Carole incredulously. "Who with?"

"No one in particular, but if I had that strong an urge, I'd probably do it. Life's too short to wonder. Besides, when you're really turned on, the other person's sex is incidental."

Carole sighed. "But if I do it, what happens if I never go back to men?"

John laughed. "You're in no danger. You like cock — I'll vouch for that." He moved closer to her. "This chick has you mesmerized with all her glamour. You'll tire of her soon. I've seen you this way about other things."

Carole said emphatically, "I'll never get tired of looking at her face. But the gay world — what I saw of it at those bars scares me."

"You won't wind up a dyke. Has Nikki ever tried anything?"

Carole remembered how easily Nikki had fallen asleep on her lap. "No. And I sure gave her a good opportunity."

"Does she know how you feel about her?" John asked.

"I don't think she knows . . . everything."

John persisted. "What do you think that bar tour was all about? Quit playing games. At least talk to her about it."

CHAPTER ELEVEN

For a week Carole worked long frenzied hours developing, printing, cropping, enlarging the pictures of Nikki and the ocelot. She saw how Nikki's hands caressed the fur of the animal, how she pursed her lips while cooing to him, how suggestively she let the animal's body drape across her breasts. She stared into the blueness of Nikki's eyes and listened to her own breathing become shallow, rapid. "You're so beautiful," she said aloud to an 11" by 14" image.

Gazing at the drying prints hanging in her darkroom, she felt enveloped by Nikki's aura. Every time she remembered Nikki's simple kiss, she was gripped in a warm liquid excitement that flowed between her thighs. She craved more.

She remembered how she had felt with John. He was good, too, she thought. But her feelings for him were less complicated, more direct. They never lingered to haunt her. And yet, sex with him was real. With her . . ."

Incessantly she replayed her conversation with John. "Life's too short to wonder. Besides, when you're really turned on, the other person's sex is incidental."

This only fueled her impulses to confront Nikki. How? she asked herself in front of the bathroom mirror. What can I possibly say to her? "Nikki, I can't stop thinking about you," she said tonelessly. "Nikki," she said dramatically, "you've possessed my every thought." "Nikki," she said with a nasal twang, "I've got the hots for ya'. Take me." She assumed an intellectual pose. "Nikki, I must talk to you about a possible homosexual experience between us."

Carole burst out laughing. "What the hell!"

She drove to Nikki's apartment. It was ten-thirty p.m. Between the time she parked and rang the doorbell, twenty additional minutes elapsed.

Nikki answered the door. Carole barged in.

"What's the matter this time?" Nikki whispered.

"Why are you whispering?" Carole demanded. "Is *she* here?" Nikki nodded and tiptoed over to close the bedroom door.

Carole paced. "I need to talk to you, now. But not with her here." Her agitation built. Then she bolted for the front door.

Nikki caught her arm, steered her into the kitchen. She forcefully sat her down. "Wait here. I'll be right back."

"Never mind," Carole said. "It's my fault. I should have called."

"Stay there, Carole."

Sitting alone in the kitchen, her hands shaking, Carole was overcome by embarrassment. She heard voices rising from the bedroom. She knew she would be unable to say anything to Nikki. Quickly, quietly, she escaped.

Trudging up the stairs to her apartment she was intercepted by Cristina who was out walking the ocelot.

"You're out late, Carole. Anything wrong? You seem upset."

Carole impatiently answered, "I'm okay."

"How's your girlfriend Mickey? Did the pictures turn out?"

"She's not my girlfriend," shouted Carole, slamming into her apartment.

Entering the darkroom, she heard a light knock at the door. She went to answer it, hastily constructing an apology to Cristina.

"May I come in?" Nikki was dressed in tight white pants and a white turtleneck sweater.

Carole stood aside to let her enter. "Come see the prints of you with the ocelot." She tried to keep firm control over her voice.

"It's really dark," said Nikki. "I feel like I'm backstage."

Carole laughed nervously. "The safelight does give off an eerie feeling. Your eyes will soon get used to the red."

Standing close to each other, they slowly looked through Carole's work. Nikki's perfume permeated the darkness.

Nikki took the pictures out of Carole's hands and looked at them closely. Her eyes widened as she saw herself highlighted in a seemingly endless portfolio. "These are wonderful! But you didn't come to see me about these pictures, did you?"

Rattled by her directness, Carole stammered, "I — I'm not sure I can talk about it now."

"Try." Nikki handed the pictures back to her. "And let's get out of this cubbyhole. The smell's too strong for me."

"All I can smell is your perfume," answered Carole. "It's stronger than all my chemicals combined."

Nikki laughed softly. "It's Jungle Gardenia. I'll wait for you in the other room."

Carole hurriedly cleaned up the darkroom and joined Nikki. "I didn't expect to see you so soon. What did you do about —"

"That's my business," Nikki interrupted. "I came to invite you to the beach."

"Now?" asked Carole, alarmed.

"I have the keys to a friend's house. He's not using it tonight. Get a coat. I'll drive." Nikki picked up Carole's purse and keys and opened the front door and waited.

Outside, Cristina was coming back with Elsker. "Hi, Carole," she called cautiously. "Hi, Mickey."

"Nice to see you Cristina," said Nikki. "I just saw the pictures. They're quite good." She stopped to pet the ocelot, then took hold of Carole's hand and led her toward the Chrysler.

They drove north for an hour before turning off Pacific Coast Highway and onto a narrow private road which led to a large darkened beach house. Nikki opened the trunk and pulled out an overnight case. The implications of the suitcase made Carole squirm; but the ease of Nikki's movements quelled her fears.

She followed Nikki into the house, and watched her deftly turn off the alarm system. Nikki flipped a master switch, and lamps throughout the round spacious living room came on.

"My God! That's a Matisse," exclaimed Carole.

Floodlights on top of the house illuminated crashing waves, their spray rising wildly into the night. Nikki held her hand out to Carole and walked her over to the large bay window. "Night is my favorite time here."

"I can see why," uttered Carole.

"The owner is a good friend of mine," explained Nikki. "I stay here sometimes when he's not using it. Why don't you look around? I'll open a bottle of wine."

"Don't you think it's awfully cold in here?" asked Carole to excuse her shiver of nervousness.

"The house warms quickly," said Nikki as she went to a small galley kitchen.

Carole moved over to the record collection. Rows of albums — Duke Ellington, Ella Fitzgerald, Peggy Lee, Anita O'Day, Stan Kenton. "What, no David Bowie? I saw him last October. He was terrific." Carole filed through the albums. "Doesn't this guy like anything modern?"

"He says he only listens to vintage music."

"These tables look hand-carved. Where are they from?"

"Indonesia. They're his pride and joy." Nikki pulled the cork from a bottle of wine.

A white envelope with Nikki's name written on it rested on a table. Carole hefted the envelope. Feels like money, she thought.

"Here, let me take that," said Nikki. She calmly dropped the envelope into her purse.

She filled two glasses with white wine, then moved toward the couch and patted the cushion invitingly. "The wine will relax you," she said.

Carole took two big gulps. "God, I hope so."

"What did you want to talk about, Carole?"

"You always get to it before I'm ready. It all started with something John said."

"Him again."

Carole paused. "I'm afraid so. He blames you for ruining my relationship with him."

"And what do you think?"

"At first, no. Now, I'm not sure. He thinks you and I have a thing going."

Carole looked for some sign of confirmation. Nikki remained silent.

"John said there was nothing wrong with it," Carole added hurriedly. "He said he's even thought about it for himself."

"How adventurous," said Nikki evenly.

Carole took another sip of the wine. "John thinks people should follow their inclination, and let it work through their system."

"Like a virus," Nikki said caustically.

"Nikki, you're making this very difficult for me."

"Carole, I want *you* to talk to me, not through John. You and I are here alone."

Carole's throat tightened and her voice wavered. "I admitted I was attracted to you, and he said you were trying to seduce me."

Nikki sipped her wine. "Much as I hate the bastard, he's right. It might not have started out that way, but tonight I'm definitely trying to seduce you."

Carole felt the color drain from her face. She waited for Nikki to say something more. Instead, she continued to sip her wine.

Carole asked, "Is this why we're at the beach house with the wine and the whole bit?"

"I had to pick up that envelope, and no, I didn't really plan this ahead of time. I'd already packed that overnight bag. Besides, you're the one who came to me, remember?"

"Don't remind me," she pleaded.

Nikki spoke in hushed tones. "You know, Carole, nothing has to happen. Now or ever. I would never do anything to hurt you. You're the one who has to decide."

"I've already decided. I wouldn't be here if I hadn't." She paused and wished it were next year. "Is it always this awkward?"

Nikki laughed. "This is fun."

"Maybe for you. I feel like I'm going to die."

Nikki laughed again and this time Carole joined her. Then, as Carole reached for her glass, Nikki took her hand and pulled her toward her. Carole went easily, without resistance, taking refuge in Nikki's shoulder, her head resting on Nikki's soft breasts. Once there, she sighed deeply and thought: Finally.

Her heart thudding, she pressed her head deeply into Nikki's plush white sweater. No bra lay beneath. She heard Nikki's heart pulse in a slow, even cadence. She inhaled her fragrance.

Nikki stroked Carole's neck. Carole's body yearned for more. She sat up and turned to Nikki. With both hands she took Nikki's face and gazed into the tranquil blue of her eyes. She drew Nikki closer.

Carole's lips moved to the blue and then hesitatingly moved toward Nikki's full inviting mouth. It was Nikki who guided Carole's head so that their lips would meet.

Carole kissed her slowly, softly, exploringly. Gaining confidence, she kissed Nikki with greater fervor. And in turn, Nikki's response quickened. Her hands moved beneath the blouse to unfasten Carole's bra, and Carole felt her breasts fondled tenderly, her nipples rise between Nikki's fingers. Carole removed her blouse and bra, revealing herself to Nikki.

Carole reddened as Nikki gazed at her breasts. Nikki kissed each one and lightly traced the outside of the nipples with her tongue.

"I want to see you, too," whispered Carole.

Nikki drew back, pulled off her sweater.

"I love the way you look," Carole said. "Come closer to me."

Nikki rested her hands on Carole's thighs. Carole closed her eyes and envisioned Nikki's hands as they pressed gently upon her. The hands became burning coals, burrowing inward and upward through her body. Urgently Carole grasped Nikki's hands and forcefully pressed them between her legs.

Swiftly Nikki snapped open Carole's jeans, slid the zipper down. Nikki had barely entered her before Carole felt herself spinning wildly. Her body thrashed, pushing Nikki deeper into herself, a hot pressure pushing inside her. She pressed against it with abandon, pursuing her release. Then waves of pleasure overtook her.

She heard Nikki say, "Are you all right?"

Carole closed her eyes. "Wonderful," she murmured.

Nikki slipped off Carole's pants and then slowly took off her own. She walked toward Carole and lay down next to her — their bodies touched for the first time.

Overcome by the smooth softness, she pressed Nikki closer to her, hungry to know more, her body aching with urgent anticipation.

Nikki touched Carole's breasts, then lightly stoked the inside of her thighs. "More, Nikki," Carole urged. She opened her legs, and Nikki lowered her head between them. "Yes," said Carole, and raised herself eagerly to meet her.

As Nikki burrowed further into her, Carole felt herself climbing higher and higher. As Nikki's lips and tongue explored her, Carole's universe became smaller, tighter, louder, until she relinquished all control and surrendered to ecstasy.

Exhausted, she lay on the couch with Nikki's head against her. Acutely aware that she had not yet touched Nikki, she carefully placed her hand between Nikki's legs. Nikki stopped her.

"I want to make love to you," Carole insisted. "Let me."

Nikki kissed her lightly. "Not now. I'm still too sensitive."

"What do you mean? I never touched you."

"You didn't have to. I was excited. That happens to me sometimes."

"Explain," Carole pressed. "I want to learn."

"Morning is just a few hours away." Nikki rose and pulled Carole up with her and led her down the hall to a bedroom across from the master suite. Pulling down the comforter, they got into bed.

Nikki drew Carole closer. "Are you sleepy?"

"I feel selfish. You gave me so much."

"You gave me a great deal too," Nikki reassured her. "You're a very passionate woman." She spoke drowsily. "This has been a special night."

Carole kissed Nikki's hand. "It felt so right. You sound sleepy."

"I am — very."

Carole heard Nikki's steady breathing. I must be very calming to her, thought Carole, holding back a giggle. This is the second time she's fallen asleep on me.

She marveled at the distance she had travelled since that lonely week when the only Nikki she possessed was the one in those darkroom photos.

The pang of morning-after anxiety disappeared when she opened her eyes and saw Nikki looking at her with affection. She reached over and playfully pulled one of Nikki's curls. "I wish I could tell you I had the most wonderful dream last night, but the truth is I slept like a rock — a happy rock."

Nikki laughed. "What a lovely thing to say. I love hearing happiness in your voice." She took Carole's hand and kissed it.

Carole's arms were outstretched. "Nestle up close. I love the way your body feels next to mine."

Nikki moved upward until her breasts pressed against Carole. Carole's palms traced the firm outline of Nikki's back. She heard Nikki's breathing quicken and felt her own heart race.

Carole opened her legs. She enclosed Nikki's firm buttocks and pressed Nikki's hips against her own. She felt the soft warmth of Nikki's kisses — kisses that by their ardor spurred Carole to reach down and probe into the waiting moistness of Nikki.

Her mouth on Nikki's, Carole slowly turned until Nikki's body rested beneath her. Nikki guided her lips to her breasts and Carole's mouth enveloped Nikki's nipples, her tongue brushing them erect.

Enraptured by Nikki's response, Carole felt every fiber of her being rise in an altogether new passionate hunger, and she unleashed herself upon the accepting Nikki.

Carole loved Nikki's body with her eyes, her hands and with her mouth. As if from a distance, she heard Nikki's cries. "More . . . yes . . . Oh, God, Yes Carole . . ." She savored, caressed, kissed, and then drank until a long violent tremor from Nikki's body forced her to stop.

Her head nestled between Nikki's legs, Carole was suffused with satiety bordering on intoxication.

"Be with me," urged Nikki in a low voice. She led Carole to the pillow next to her. "I love the way you took me."

Carole lay on her back, closed her eyes and tried to steady the heat pulsing through her body. She couldn't. "Nikki, please touch me."

Nikki hovered over her, and with both hands slowly stroking, seared Carole into climax.

CHAPTER TWELVE

The bathroom was a temple: a blue tiled sunken tub, marble wash basin with golden fixtures, mirrors paneling the walls, and built-in seats inside the shower. Carole turned the shower head to massage, and sat while torrents of warmth pulsated on her back. She wanted to stay there forever, mentally rerunning the past twenty-four hours.

Now it all made sense, she thought. It isn't the opposite sex who teaches us about ourselves. Only a woman can understand the secrets of another. Maybe self-knowledge becomes complete when we journey into ourselves through the same sex.

She opened a large mirrored door to discover high stacks of blue and purple plush towels monogrammed HD. She wrapped herself in a large sheet towel and stood before the mirror.

Perhaps I should be worried, she mused, and yet nothing has ever felt so right. Moving closer to the mirror, she opened the towel and studied her body. I look the same as before, but I feel so different. I'm changed. Strange that it doesn't show.

Caressing her breasts, she discovered that her nipples were sore. With renewed pleasure she recalled how eagerly Nikki's mouth had loved them. She was filled with an urgent desire to see her.

Wrapped in the towel, wet hair clinging to her forehead, Carole walked into the kitchen where Nikki was slicing a red ball of gouda cheese into thin ovals.

Full of love, Carole moved toward Nikki. She immediately stopped herself when Nikki looked over her shoulder and said matter-of-factly, "Oh, good, you're finished."

Chilled, bewildered, Carole stared at her. Matching Nikki's impersonal voice, she asked, "Who's HD? His initials are plastered all over the bathroom."

"This is his house. Are you hungry? I didn't feel like cooking eggs. Besides, I'm in a hurry this morning."

"Oh," said Carole bitterly disappointed. Sarcastically she added, "I guess you have better things to do. Listen, forget the cheese. I'll get dressed right away."

Nikki's tone softened. "I hear pouting in your voice. I want you to come with me to my morning date in Holmby

Park. Later on, I'm supposed to meet Janice for our regular brunch." She asked, "Why are you upset?"

"I was hoping we could talk and be together. What happened is really important to me. I don't want to rush out of here — I don't feel I can just jump into my old life as if nothing had happened. Of course," she added hurriedly, "you have no obligations to me. It's just that I feel sentimental — romantic. Where do we go from here?"

Nikki took Carole in her arms and held her comfortingly. "I don't know any more than you do. Be patient." She kissed Carole across the forehead and on the mouth. When Carole's arms tightened around her, Nikki moved away.

Nikki placed some Wheat Thins on the counter between herself and Carole. Picking up one of the cheese ovals and placing it over a cracker so that the edges overlapped, she bit the oval into a perfect square with slow precise bites.

"Carole," she said. "I care a great deal for you. I don't see this morning as the end of our friendship. I'm happy that everything happened the way it did. I truly do have errands to run this morning. Don't misconstrue this and make yourself unhappy. Come on, cheer up." She reached over and chucked Carole under the chin.

Reluctantly, Carole forced a smile. She popped a piece of cheese into her mouth. "I do lean to melodrama, especially with you. There's so much I want to ask you. Promise you'll find the time to tell me how it was with you — the first time."

Nikki laughed. "I'll tell you what I can remember. It's been so long ago."

"I could never forget," said Carole solemnly. "And I don't believe *you* have." She heard herself sounding

107

serious again, and lightened her tone, lest she appear too needy. "So, tell me about HD."

"Get dressed. I'll tell you in the car. I don't want to get caught in traffic and be late to Holmby Park."

An overcast sky loomed over the Malibu and Santa Monica beaches. Nikki sped through the clumps of fog that rested in the dips of Pacific Coast Highway.

Carole looked at the speedometer — eighty miles per hour. She can't get away fast enough, she thought. She's taking me back too soon. I'm not ready to see my place yet. I don't want to see anything I've ever seen before. Goddamn seagulls.

The Chrysler glided smoothly out of a steep dip. "Slow down. I don't want to die," Carole shouted. "Besides, you said you'd tell me about HD."

Nikki maintained the same speed. "HD stands for Humberto Donato. I call him Bert. He's one of my oldest and dearest friends."

Carole remembered the envelope with money. "Is he the one who gave you the car?"

"Yes," answered Nikki. "It was an early graduation present. When my transmission went out on my old car, he got me this."

"And in return you —"

"Everybody thinks that." Nikki's face assumed a bored expression. "I met Bert over ten years ago in a club when I was working Cleveland. I like to call him my guardian angel because he watches over me."

"Is he good looking?"

"He's a good-looking sixty-three-year-old man who likes to show off with pretty girls. He's always a gentleman. He takes me and the other dancers around to clubs here and in Las Vegas. He has a lot of connections there."

"Come on, Nikki. Level with me — nothing's for free."

Nikki nodded agreement. "It's not for free. Playing the role of grateful recipient isn't easy. It's like he needs me to need him. He finds ways for me to repay him. I keep up the beach house and run special errands."

Carole asked, "If this guy does all this stuff for you, how come you still work?"

Nikki eased up on the accelerator. "That question cuts to the quick. I don't feel like going into it right now."

Carole chuckled. "I'm going to tell you something that might make you mad. Please don't let it. When I first told John you were a stripper, he wondered if you hooked on the side."

"He's a son-of-a-bitch." Nikki's fingers tightened around the steering wheel. "Where do you get off telling me what that slime thinks about my life? I was confiding in you, Carole. Very few people know about my relationship with Bert, and that's how I want it. If I can't trust you, let me know right now."

Humiliated, Carole promised, "I'll never tell anybody. Does Bert know you're gay?"

"Absolutely. Not only does he know, he was very upset when Janice and I broke up. They're good friends to this day."

"He sounds too good to be real."

Nikki turned left onto Sunset Boulevard and they drove in comfortable silence to Holmby Park. Carole watched from inside the car as Nikki opened the trunk and pulled out two small cans and a box of aluminum foil.

"Come on," Nikki urged her.

Carole followed a few steps behind. The sun had broken though the morning clouds and its rays illuminated Nikki's hair to golden red.

They circled the putting green and walked under the covered walkway to a table in the picnic area. Nikki glanced at her watch. "Only a half hour late."

She spread a sheet of aluminum foil on the ground and opened two cans of skinless, boneless Norwegian sardines, and emptied them onto the foil. "Gypsy! Gypsy! Here, Gyp, Gyp, Gyp, Gyp!" she called in a soprano voice. She repeated her call. She looked at Carole and said under her breath, "He's torturing me."

Astonished, Carole watched her disappear into a bamboo grove still calling, "Gypsy!" Bamboo leaves clinging to her sweater and pants and hair, she soon emerged clutching a yowling, muscular black cat to her chest. Her face was radiant, triumphant.

Incredulous, Carole asked, "This is your date?"

"I think he's mad at me. Look at his face. Isn't it regal?"

"Not really." For *this* Nikki had rushed away from the aftermath of their lovemaking? "I didn't know you were into stray cats."

"I'm a stray cat myself," said Nikki. She walked back toward the picnic area and carefully placed Gypsy in front of the sardines. Then she sat on the picnic bench and watched as the cat ravenously devoured his feast. She said proudly, "In ancient Egypt there was a law that said if a house was on fire, the cat must be saved first."

Carole looked at the earnest face. She smiled. "You look very pretty right now."

"I hope you don't think I tricked you when I was vague about my date this morning. I didn't know if you'd understand. I have trouble explaining the importance of Gypsy."

"If you love him so much, why don't you take him home with you? It's mean to leave him here. Does anyone else feed him besides you?"

"I'm sure I'm not the only one who feeds him. I'm afraid to decide to own him. Something keeps me from doing that. Corny as it may sound, I envision him a free spirit."

Gypsy finished his meal, washed himself, jumped onto the picnic table and circled his way toward Nikki. He put his head down and she scratched it. Little by little, he came closer until he rested peacefully in her lap. She closed her eyes and rested her back against the wooden table, and cradled the cat. Gypsy purred loudly, then stretched and curled himself into a sleeping crescent.

CONTACT PRINT VI

Calumet City — 1950

During the Korean War, Janice was friends with the bartender who always drove her home when the Bali Hai Club closed.

One night the bartender said to her, "Sorry Janice, I can't take you tonight."

"Don't worry about it. I'll take a cab."

A young soldier who had been sitting at the bar overheard their conversation, walked over shyly, and politely offered to drive her. Strippers had been told to be nice to servicemen, and warned never to roll them. Janice preferred to avoid them altogether. But she reconsidered when the bartender winked at her as if to say the soldier was all right.

After driving a few miles, he pulled into a motel parking lot.

"Oh no!" she protested, moving away from him.

"Oh yes!"

He grinned, then suddenly grabbed her by her blouse and punched her. The blow broke all her front teeth. He forced one hand down her blouse and the other up her skirt.

"At least open the door and let me spit these teeth out," she pleaded.

He let her, and she rolled out of the car and ran toward a nearly-finished housing development. He pursued her in the car. She crawled into the cellar of an unfinished house, hiding in terror as she heard the car tracking her up and down the dirt streets. He left at dawn.

Later that morning, Janice was admitted into the hospital to have her teeth pulled. Two days later, with a new set of teeth and a mouthful of stitches, she ordered a steak dinner.

"As long as they're going to be part of me, I might as well get used to them right now."

CHAPTER THIRTEEN

Nikki had arrived late for her customary brunch with Janice at Natural Path, a fashionable health food restaurant in Century City.

Janice had taken a liking to Natural Path, because unlike other health food places, it permitted smoking. The entire center had been architecturally designed to promote a feeling of glamour; here consumers could purchase Taiwan-made apparel and still feel affluent.

Janice was forty-two. She was a handsome, large-framed woman who moved with a slow grace. Her dominant feature was her green eyes, deep-set, almost Asian in their shape. Her short, wavy hair had known many shades, but for the last five years ash blonde had softened the lines encroaching around her eyes and mouth.

"I didn't say you look sick," said Janice for the second time in a pronounced Louisiana drawl, "I just said you looked pale. Maybe it's because you don't have any makeup on."

Nikki raised her voice. "Look, I've already put in a full day, and it's barely eleven o'clock. If I look that terrible, then don't look at me."

Janice laughed softly. "I'd forgotten how many freckles you have. Makes you look young." She cautioned, "But you can't deny your years or the life you've led. This girl sounds too straight and she may be too young."

"I'm hardly robbing the cradle," Nikki insisted. "I can only meet women at work or school. The lesbians I meet at bars — that I like — are Carole and Lorayne's age, but they either want to play the field or they've already settled down."

The pink-dressed waitress served Nikki eggs benedict and placed a spinach and mushroom omelette before Janice. Janice ignored her food and stared at Nikki as if waiting for some further explanation. She waited until Nikki had eaten one of the eggs before asking, "You sure you don't like younger ones because they're just easier?"

"No. There's just more of them available. Carole's different. I think she may come to love me for myself — eventually. I don't want to rush things with her. I want the relationship to mature slowly. I want her to get to know me — the real me."

115

"Listen here," Janice warned, "there's no future in a young one, Nikki. She'll be sure to leave you."

Nikki pushed her empty plate away. "Honey, you were the older one, and *you* left me. Remember?"

"Every time I see you," Janice answered. She added, "Since we broke up you've never had any lasting relationship. The older you are, the harder it'll be to find someone. Now you've broken up with Lorayne who replaced Andi, who replaced Dorothy. Should I go on?"

Nikki shook her head vehemently. "Can the lecture. My needs are different from yours. You've got June, your house, your job. I've got to finish school. I haven't had time for something permanent. I waited too long to get out of stripping."

"Well," Janice drawled. "I never thought I'd hear you admit that. Regardless, you're going to need someone, sugar pie. By the time you settle down, only the crumbs'll be left."

Nikki teased, "You're mothering again."

Janice reached into her purse and took out a package of Marlboros. With precision she opened the pack and transferred its contents into a worn silver case. As she laid out her cigarettes, her eyes fell on the inscription: *Don't ever forget that I love you. Nikki. 1965.*

Janice looked up at her. "I can't help it." She reached over and soothingly patted Nikki's hand. "I think your fear of settling down is partly my fault."

"Maybe it has been — in the past."

Janice smiled wryly and sang, "This could be the start of something big..."

"Don't laugh at me, Janice. Meet her first. There's something delightful about Carole." She smiled. "The others were strippers, actresses, competitors of mine in some way. She's an artist — a wonderful photographer —

116

and she talks about her feelings." Nikki hesitated. "She makes me want to talk about mine. I like that. I've never done that before, except with you. I even told her about Bert."

Janice motioned the waitress to clear off the table. She leaned forward and warned, "I wouldn't talk about Bert's business to anybody. As for your schoolgirl, how do you know you're not some kind of experiment?"

"Because of all the girls I've brought out, she was sure of what she wanted — me. Only me. What's more, in the morning she didn't play the 'you made me do it' game. She was so overflowing with love I didn't know how to handle it."

"It's good you're going slowly with her," said Janice and asked for the check.

They strolled the store-studded square. Janice waited while Nikki shopped for books. Then they walked to Nikki's favorite dress shop, where they were warmly greeted by the pretty head saleslady who immediately brought out the newest arrivals.

"As soon as I unpacked this blazer, I thought of you and your lovely red hair." She smiled enthusiastically, deep dimples accentuating her delight. She waved a rust-colored jacket, and held it up against Nikki's chest.

Kay had thick salt and pepper hair worn in a stylish chignon. She was part of Janice and Nikki's Saturday ritual.

Janice was never friendly toward Kay. "Dimples on middle-aged women look obscene," she had once said to Nikki. Janice also had her own theory about this overly-friendly, solicitous woman who always made it her business to be in the close-quartered dressing room when Nikki disrobed.

117

"I'd just love to paint you," Kay had once whispered to Nikki.

Later, Janice had told Nikki, "She's gotta be the oldest closet case in Century City."

But Kay was a ritual, and Janice and Nikki had come to enjoy the weekly sexually-covert transactions between Nikki and Kay.

A loud horn woke up Carole. She had dozed off at a red light on her way to John's apartment in Santa Monica.

I should have stayed home and gotten more sleep, she thought. I don't want to see him, but I need to talk to someone.

In her mind's eye she saw the innocent picture of Gypsy curled on Nikki's lap. Yet, she realized that the person she now loved would also inevitably expose her to aspects of life she might not like.

She remembered her promise not to talk about Nikki's relationship with Bert. She hasn't told me the whole story. What if she's Bert's mistress?

To herself she whispered, "For you, Nikki, I'll abandon everything — the familiar, the safe."

John asked, grinning, "Well, was it better with her than with me?"

Carole frowned. "I knew you'd ask."

"Was it?"

"I feel very — complete," she said simply.

The kettle whistled and John turned off the burner. "The only tea I have is Red Zinger." He laughed. "Seems appropriate talking about Nikki."

Carole smiled. The chip on her shoulder lightened.

He carried two mugs with floating red tea bags onto the plant-filled balcony and set them on a small telephone wire spool he had converted into a patio table. He picked up the tea bag and gingerly dipped it in and out of the water. "Tell me how you're more complete."

She looked at his hands as they toyed with his drink. She had loved his hands — the tops delicate, almost feminine, the palms calloused, rough from gardening and woodworking.

She couldn't tell him anything, she realized. "I didn't feel strange making love, or afterwards. I guess that's the main thing I have to say."

"That doesn't tell me why you're more complete," he pressed sarcastically. "If you don't want to describe what you and Nikki did, then why did you drive all the way out here? I think you're trying to provoke me."

She shook her head and in exasperation ran her hands through her hair. "I came because I had no one else to talk to. I can see this isn't going to work — you're more concerned with the sexual details. It wasn't lurid John, it was wonderful. What I feel now is more than I've ever felt before with anyone. It's sexuality, sensuality, and everything else that goes with those words."

He raised his brows in mock surprise. "Ah, so you're dividing sexuality and sensuality? A bit of Erich Fromm?"

"John, attaching some author's ideas to my feelings doesn't make them less unique. I'm not trying to get you mad," she said tiredly. "I came to talk to what I thought was a friend. I was wrong. Now there's nothing between us."

He leaned back in his chair and sipped his tea.

"All I know is, I want to be with her."

John chuckled. "Are you sure it's her and not just girls in general? Maybe you've been latent all your life."

119

Anger built inside Carole. She rose and leaned against the railing. "You're putting me down for being honest. To think I was naive enough to believe you were my friend. You're pathetic. I feel sorry for you."

His face was deadpan. "Finished now? If there's pity to be thrown around, it should land in your front yard. You don't know who or what you are. You're always jumping on the latest bandwagon — peace marches, dope, meditation, and now chicks."

Carole picked up her purse. "Truthfully, I think you're jealous. You wish you could have seen the show."

"Sorry to disappoint you, honey. But watching dykes going at it would leave my cock limp."

She opened the door and turned to him and said in mock seriousness, "Windy days do that to you too."

She slammed the door behind her, the sound signaling with finality the ending of that part of her life.

Nikki's face filled her thoughts. As she thought of Nikki's unknown world before her, Carole's mood lightened; excitement filled her. John's right, she thought, I do follow bandwagons.

CHAPTER FOURTEEN

Efforts to accomplish anything in the darkroom proved fruitless. All Carole could see was Nikki. Losing patience, she abandoned her work and flopped onto the bed. She shut her eyes as tightly as possible, but even then there was too much light filtering through her eyelids. She picked up the pillow and laid it over her face. Perfect.

In slow motion she replayed the events of the previous evening, starting with Nikki pouring the wine, next hearing Nikki admit that she was trying to seduce her. Carole's heart raced as she again felt Nikki's breasts against her face, and then in a freeze-frame she re-lived her first taste of Nikki's warm vulnerable mouth.

Carole heard herself moan. She threw the pillow from her face. Her breathing quickened as she became aware of her pulsing wetness. She unfastened her pants and moved her hand down, all the time visualizing how Nikki's long fingers had caressed her into frenzy.

"Nikki! Nikki!" she called. She peaked immediately.

Jesus, what's happening to me? She looked down and saw her hand wedged between her legs. Feeling empty and foolish, she ripped off her clothes and showered.

"I have to make her love me. She has to love me," Carole said to herself. She was going through her wardrobe, making two piles of clothing, one for the Salvation Army, the other for the cleaners. She assessed her taste in clothes and found it shabby compared to Nikki's.

"I'll make her take me shopping." She made a mental note to write her father at his office to let him know that she was going to use his credit card again.

Clothes won't do it, she thought. My hair, my crazy frizzy hair. What will she think when it rains and it's standing on end?

The sound of the ringing phone startled her.

"What are you doing?"

Nikki's voice threw Carole into a panic. Carole said faintly, "Oh, nothing. Aren't you at work?"

"Yes, and thinking of you."

"Nikki, I'm doing the same thing," she blurted, and immediately regretted her honesty.

"Can you come for my last show and then go out to breakfast? Bert's taking all the girls to Dino's."

A slight disappointment arose in Carole. "I want to be with you — won't I be an outsider?"

"You'll be with me. Besides, I already told him all about you."

"You did?" Carole wondered how she had been described. "*All* about me?"

Nikki laughed softly. "I kept the best parts to myself. Can you be here around one-thirty?"

"Of course."

Tall, thin, olive-skinned, dressed in a dark three-piece suit, Bert walked directly to Carole's table. "You're Carole," he said politely and extended his hand. "I'm Humberto Donato — Bert."

Carole sat up straight and stiffly shook his hand. "How do you do?"

"May I join you?" He smiled and sat down before she could answer. As strains of *Mademoiselle de Paris* came over the sound system, Bert prompted, "Ah! There's Nikki's intro."

Relieved that there was no time for small talk, Carole, her stomach in knots, turned attentively toward the stage. He knows, she thought. He knows about me. Is he comparing me to Lorayne? Shit, I hope not.

She forced herself to concentrate on Nikki and noticed that tonight she seemed to dance with extra vitality, moving provocatively, sensually, playing directly to their table.

Curious, Carole leaned back to see how Bert reacted to Nikki's tease. He threw back his head and laughed when she aimed a quick and accentuated bump at him. His pleasure seemed more fatherly than anything else. He obviously enjoyed watching her, but there was no evidence of sexual interest.

When Nikki disrobed and deftly removed her corselette without missing a beat, he commented, "When I first met her in Cleveland, she'd go off stage to do that."

Carole failed to appreciate the smoothness of the strip. All she saw was the pear-shaped beauty of Nikki's breasts. Carole picked up her drink, fearful that her reddening face might betray the excitement she felt.

How unfair, she thought. After making love to her, this is where I see her body again. It's cruel.

Nikki's dance ended and as she came forward for an extra bow, Carole clapped perfunctorily.

Bert turned to Carole, elated. "After all these years I never tire of seeing her."

"Has she changed very much?"

"Better. Always her dancing is better. Never vulgar." He took Carole's hand. "I would like to see the pictures you took of her with the tiger. She said you're a true artist."

Carole blushed. "I'll give Nikki a set for you." Her mind raced to think of something ingratiating to say.

The house lights came on, signaling the end of the evening, and as the patrons exited from the club two waitresses served magnums of Dom Perignon in frosted silver buckets to Bert's table.

Dressed in street clothes, three strippers, chatting loudly, came from backstage and joined Carole and Bert. Each of them kissed him ceremoniously on both cheeks.

"Look at him. He never ages," purred Precious Pearl to Lotus Linn and Dreamy Daniels.

"Where have you been hiding?" asked Dreamy, softly stroking his arm. "We've missed having you around."

"Busy with business. But never too busy to breakfast with beautiful friends."

Carole saw that he acknowledged their attentions matter-of-factly — a man accustomed to tribute.

"Sit down, girls," Bert ordered. "I'm pouring."

The dancers giggled excitedly. "This is what I love about you, Bert. Nothing but the best," squealed Lotus.

What a bunch of kiss-asses, Carole thought scornfully.

Bert turned to her and asked, "Champagne?" He poured without waiting for her answer. "Have you ladies met Carole?"

"You're Nikki's new girlfriend, right?" asked Lotus. "She'll be out in a few minutes. She's back there with Torchy."

"Torchy's really blazing tonight," muttered Dreamy Daniels.

"Amen!" said Pearl.

Bert turned to the dancers. "Carole's a wonderful photographer."

Carole felt uncomfortable with the compliment. "I go to school with Nikki," she said hastily.

"Do you do publicity pictures? I'm tired of cosmetology school. I'm thinking of going into commercials. I need a composite," Lotus said.

Carole felt all eyes upon her. "I do portraits, but not composites."

A voice boomed across the room: "There better be some champagne left for me!"

Torchy weaved across the empty club, a harried Nikki trying unsuccessfully to keep her steady.

The dancers groaned and exchanged knowing glances. Bert stood, tried to guide Torchy to a chair. She spurned him, pulled up her own chair, snatched Dreamy's glass and downed its contents. She yanked the champagne bottle from the bucket and refilled her glass. The other dancers pointedly ignored her.

Nikki extended her hand to Bert and he kissed it. He slid over to the next chair allowing Nikki to sit beside Carole.

Nikki reached for Carole's hand under the table. Carole whispered, "Where have you been?"

"Trying to calm down my friend." Nikki squeezed Carole's hand. "I'm so glad you're here."

They all jumped at a loud crash. Torchy had fallen off her chair, turning over the ice bucket.

Awestruck, no one did anything as champagne soaked into the carpet. Finally, Bert stood and announced, "I'm famished. How about breakfast?"

One by one the women rose and moved toward the door — all except Torchy, who was trying to get up off the floor.

"That's right," she slurred angrily. "You all had your fill, so now you're ready to go."

"Stay if you want," said Bert. "We're going to Dino's." To Nikki and Carole he said, "Ride with me."

From the door Lotus called, "We'll meet you there."

Nikki and Carole followed a solemn-faced Bert out to a caramel-colored Bentley. He opened the door for them and as he walked to the driver's side Carole quickly asked Nikki, "Is he mad?"

"Very," nodded Nikki. "He hates scenes."

As Bert started to pull away, something struck the front of his car with a loud thud. He slammed on the brakes, throwing Nikki and Carole against the dashboard.

An angry, grimacing, florid face glared at them through the windshield. Torchy had thrown herself fully over the hood of the car, her hand clutching the antenna.

She bellowed, "I'm going with you." She took the antenna violently and banged on the windshield.

Bert lowered the window. "Get off, Torchy."

"Let me in! Tell him to let me in, Nikki. I've been a good friend to you."

"Bert," said Nikki, "people are staring. Let me talk to her. She's been a hassle all night — heavy problems with Dan."

Nikki got out of the car. Slowly she approached the straddled Torchy. "Hey, Torch. You're out of control." She put her hand over Torchy's and tried to pry her fingers from the antenna.

"Don't even try, Nik." Torchy threatened. I can toss you across the lot with one hand."

Nikki took hold of Torchy's shoulders. Torchy swung wildly, knocking her to the ground.

Bert and Carole jumped out of the car at the same time.

"Hold on to me," Carole said, helping her up. To Torchy she growled, "You disgusting bitch! And you call yourself a friend?"

"What do you know about anything, you little dyke!"

Carole let go of Nikki, grabbed Torchy's ankle, and with furious energy yanked her off the car. Torchy's head struck the fender. She landed face down on the asphalt.

Torchy lay perfectly still. Carole, breathless, stood cautiously over the woman, expecting to erupt again. Carole leaned over her, waiting. Worried, she asked, "Are you okay?"

The blow across Carole's mouth sent her reeling back. "Does that answer your question?" Torchy sneered from where she sat on the pavement.

"Bitch!" Nikki screamed, lunging between Carole and Torchy.

127

Bert roared, "Both of you, get in the car." To Torchy he held up a menacing finger. "Leave. Now."

"Not because you tell me to." Torchy got up and pulled her clothes into place. "Why do you always fuss over that piss-elegant dyke? I mean, I know you owe her one . . ."

He looked into the woman's bloodshot eyes. "Get in your car, Torchy. Your act's over. Over."

Understanding registered in Torchy's eyes. The woman sighed deeply, then staggered toward her car. As she opened the door she wheeled around and gestured with her middle finger and yelled, "Use *this* with her, you two-bit thug! Act big as you want, but I remember how you got your start!" She revved her engine, then sped away.

Bert waited until Torchy was gone before starting his car. "You girls all right?"

Nikki nodded and turned to Carole. "Are you?"

Carole held out her trembling hands. "I don't know if I'm shaking because I'm mad or scared."

Nikki took hold of Carole's hands. "I'm so sorry. I knew she was coming unglued, I had no idea she'd get this crazy. I should've forced her to go home earlier."

"You're not responsible for that drunk," said Carole angrily. "I'm sorry I didn't punch her out." She fingered her bruised lips. "Let's sue her."

Nikki and Bert smiled faintly. "For what?" Bert asked. "I say let's forget about it."

"I'll never forgive her for hitting you," she said to Carole and pressed her cheek next to hers.

Minutes later Bert escorted Nikki and Carole to a back table at Dino's where Dreamy, Lotus, and Pearl sat waiting.

"More trouble with Torchy?" asked Pearl, eyeing the disheveled Nikki and Carole.

"None whatsoever," said Bert lightly. "Let's order the usual." He called the waiter over. "The *special* orange juice . . ." The girls giggled. "Melon and prosciutto, and eggs benedict." Bert turned his attention to the dancers.

Carole was angry and exhausted. A dull pain pulsed in her head, a sharp pain stung her lips. She removed an ice cube from the water glass and pressed it to her mouth. She looked at Nikki, whose hair was barely tousled. Are you worth all this trouble? she asked herself. She looked at her watch. It was close to three a.m.

Nikki whispered, "We'll sleep in tomorrow. Let me see your mouth." Nikki put her arm around Carole.

Involuntarily, Carole pulled away. Confusion crossed Nikki's face. She drew her arm back. "I'm sorry," said Carole. "I'm not used to it. It's too much for me tonight."

"Carole, this was a terrible night. Believe me."

"The first time we went out, I got hassled in a bar. Tonight I got hit on the mouth. Nikki, you're a liability. What next?"

"Warmth and love and caring — if you'll let me."

Carole scanned the other three dancers. They were detailing their troubles about jobs, husbands, lovers, children to Bert. If you really strip them down, she thought, no matter how they act on stage they're just like other women.

The waiter brought the orange juice in large goblets. Carole had taken three gulps before she realized that it was spiked with champagne. Alarmed, she turned to Nikki.

Nikki winked playfully at Carole. "I was going to warn you to slow down. You're not used to it, remember?"

Placated, Carole rested her head on Nikki's shoulder. "You can put your arm back now," she said.

As Carole sipped her drink, her exhaustion was replaced by a mellow warmth that softened her feelings about where she was and why.

For the rest of the morning, while Bert presided over the other dancers, Carole was content to let Nikki shower her with constant attention. She wished she could make her moments among these night people last forever.

CHAPTER FIFTEEN

Carole and Nikki attended school together, and in the evenings Carole followed Nikki to the club. She was always in the corner reserved for dancers and their special friends or relatives. She no longer paid any cover charge — she had become one of the regulars, her name always on the comp list.

After hours, she was backstage chatting, visiting with the dancers. She learned that behind the dancers' glamorous facades were tawdry melodramas — cheating husbands, runaway kids, repossessed cars, fruitless auditions. Carole noticed that Nikki never talked about her own private life.

Their lovemaking was frequent, passionate, Nikki responding generously to Carole's hunger to fully realize this new realm of love. But despite their closeness in bed, Nikki rarely spoke about herself, particularly her family history, while Carole never stopped sharing anecdotes about her successful Oregon Wolston clan, and growing up Jewish. She enjoyed her role as storyteller, and would have liked to hear similar stories from her lover. She was bothered by Nikki's need for privacy and found it exasperating.

One lazy Sunday morning over breakfast, Carole decided to pursue her curiosity. "I want to know more about you."

The white fish, raw onions, baily rolls, cream cheese, Greek olives, and green pickled tomatoes that Carole had just bought were set out for them. Eyes wide, Nikki pointed to the green tomatoes. "Is this how you're going to force it out of me? I thought I'd satisfied you."

"You did. Sit down. I'm going to feed you a real Jewish breakfast. Ever had one?"

"Just lox and bagels. Is this a test?" Nikki popped an olive into her mouth.

"In a way," admitted Carole. "Nikki, I have to be honest about something."

"Oh, no," groaned Nikki good humoredly. "Here we go again."

"You might think this is stupid, but indulge me." Carole cleared her throat. "You don't *seem* Jewish. You don't act it — and you just don't *feel* it. Don't look at me that way," she said defensively. "It's just that I can always tell — and according to my antenna, you aren't." Relieved, she sighed. "There, I said it."

"Why haven't you mentioned this before?" Nikki patted her knees, motioning Carole to sit on her lap. She said gently, "I'll tell you a story."

Carole balanced herself clumsily on Nikki's lap. "I always feel like I'm going to crush you when I do this."

Nikki's arms tightened around her waist. "I didn't find out about being Jewish until a few years ago, and only then by accident. I found my grandmother's naturalization papers. Under place of birth it said Russia —"

Carole jumped up. "Russia! That's where we're from. What part?"

Nikki laughed and motioned Carole to a chair. "I think it was Odessa."

"We're from Bialystock. That's where the bailys come from. Finish the story. You didn't know before that?"

"Mom had always told me we were French and Irish. I never questioned it because of my coloring. Her maiden name is Tauber. I use it because it's different. Sounds more elegant than Halloran, my dad's name. Anyway, she never told me I was Jewish."

Carole wrinkled her nose in disapproval. "My family's always taken pride in our heritage. And I do too, even if I don't practice the faith."

"Don't be so quick to judge," Nikki snapped. "You don't know enough. My mother was born in L.A. but my grandmother dumped her in a Jewish orphanage. She stayed there until she was fifteen."

Shocked, Carole stammered, "Why would her mother abandon her?"

"She had dreams of becoming a singer, and the man she was with didn't want a child on the road with them." Sadly, Nikki added, "My mom was only eight years old."

Carole heard the anger and pain in her voice. "You don't have to continue."

Nikki covered her eyes with her hand and bowed her head. Carole put her arms around her. "I didn't know it would be so painful. I'm sorry."

Nikki wiped the tears from her cheeks with a paper napkin. "Every time I think of her alone I imagine her terror. She had no one. Can you imagine that? Having no one?" She burst into tears.

Carole knelt before her. "Stop, please. I've made a mess of things with my nosiness."

Nikki straightened. She cleared her throat. "I don't know what came over me. I'm all right now." She stood and moved to another chair — one further away from Carole. In a low voice she continued, "Anyway, it was during the thirties, and there was a lot of anti-Semitism. She ran away and found work as a mother's helper — and learned it was a lot easier not to be a Jew."

Cautiously, Carole asked, "Were you mad when she told you? I mean, how did you feel about Jews?"

Nikki motioned with her hand to slow down. "One question at a time. You mean, was I anti-Semitic? No. And no, I couldn't be mad at Mom. She was crying when she told me. She begged my forgiveness." Nikki's voice cracked. "It was the closest moment we ever had between us." She looked up at Carole and said, "I think this is enough now."

Carole looked at the food and shook her head. "I don't think eating white fish can make anyone feel Jewish, but I'm sure feeling guilty. Should we put things away and go out for ham and eggs?"

"Nonsense," said Nikki. "Heat the goddamn bialys."

This story had answered one of Carole's questions. Now she wanted to meet Janice — but as yet, she had not been included in that relationship.

Nikki had maintained her inviolate Saturday appointments: her trip to visit Gypsy, the stray cat which despite Carole's arguments Nikki refused to bring home, and her brunch date with Janice. Because Nikki always went alone, Carole still felt like an outsider.

Nikki did begin to invite some of her friends to meet Carole. These informal pot-luck evenings were always nerve-wracking, because invariably someone would ask Nikki about Lorayne, and invariably Carole would find herself blushing hotly. Nikki simply ignored the question.

Carole could not help but wonder if she was just one more stop in Nikki's life.

Though threatened by the specter of Lorayne, Carole came to enjoy the conversation of the gay women in Nikki's apartment. She sought the difference that would distinguish them from straight women. The most common phrase that emerged was "coming out."

She learned that among newly acquainted friends the inevitable question was, "When did you come out?" The question was eagerly answered, dramatically told, and duly applauded. No narrator ever appeared unprepared; each story sparkled with details complete with elaborate setting, cast of characters, conflict, and always, the implied happy ending.

Carole's favorite coming out story, however, did not come from Nikki's female friends, but from Patrick, a small, trim, attractive middle-aged man who had large expressive hazel eyes and a neatly shaped Vandyke beard.

Patrick was Nikki's oldest friend — next to Janice. It was at his elegant house in the Los Feliz district that Carole first heard Nikki say, "This is my girlfriend, Carole." When Carole's face flushed, he only remarked, "Lovely coloring," and handed her silverware and cups so that she could help him set the table.

Patrick was a mortician who moonlighted as a hairdresser and periodically cut Nikki's hair. He and his lover, Gil, had been together fifteen years. Gratefully, Carole noticed that unlike Nikki's other friends Patrick made no reference to Lorayne or other past lovers. She also noted that his conversation, thought incessant, was not centered around what couple had broken up and who was seeing whom. He spoke with wit and knowledge about literature, Watergate, Vietnam, and Zubin Mehta. Carole decided that his flighty affectations were an act. Behind the arching eyebrows and fluttering hands was an intelligent, discriminating mind worth attending to.

When he heard that Carole was from the northwest, he asked if she knew of local Indian artists who specialized in mask-making. "I had some Alaskan Indian masks made of caribou. But one day I noticed the eyebrows were moving. They were infested with parasites!"

Chuckling, Carole said, "My mother knows everything about the local tribes." She added, "She applauds Marlon Brando's stand at the Academy Awards."

Patrick grew serious. "I agree with your mother. The massacre of one hundred and twenty-five Indians at Wounded Knee is as bad as My Lai." Patrick added bitterly, "An Indian's lucky if he lives to be forty-five."

Nikki turned to Carole. "If you ever need depressing statistics, ask Patrick. His heroes are Brando and Jane Fonda."

"Somebody's got to protect us against Nixon and Governor Reagan," he said. "The country's too right-wing for me. Enough of this," he said, waving his arm dramatically. "Let's make Nikki beautiful."

Nikki had warned Carole ahead of time; "Get ready for a real show. No one does a comb-out like Patrick."

Still, Carole was not prepared for the sight of Nikki lying on a table with her head hanging over the edge, while Patrick, on his knees, meticulously cut, styled, and brushed her hair.

"Carole!" Patrick shouted. "I'd love to photograph your face right now. You're in early *rigor*. Close your mouth, dear, and let me do you next," he offered.

"Oh, no," stammered Carole. "I'm fine. I-I-I've just never seen anything like this. It's pretty funny," she said seriously.

"And you're a marvelous audience. I would consider it my pleasure to do you over. I promise you'll be happy."

Nikki urged, "Try it, honey. He's very good."

Too embarrassed to say no, Carole acquiesced. She tolerated the steaming towels, the mask, the eyebrow plucking, and his painstaking make-up application. However, she sat straight up at the sound of his rapidly snapping scissors.

"Relax. You have it easy," comforted Patrick. "When I first started doing hair on *live ones,* I couldn't comb-out unless they were lying on satin sheets. Finished, dear."

Carole smiled into the mirror with delight. "Is that really me? Patrick, you're marvelous. No more beauty

137

parlors for me — I'll take a mortician any day. What do you think, Nikki?"

"You look beautiful," said Nikki. She kissed Carole and embraced Patrick.

Two hours later, after sipping several cups of Earl Gray tea, Carole no longer thought of Patrick as a mortician but as a close friend, so close that she unwittingly asked, "Patrick, how did you come out?"

"Sweetheart, I was *born out*. My better story is how I got to the mortuary. Should I tell her, Nikki?" Without waiting for an answer, he continued, stroking his small beard as he spoke. "When I was fifteen my father tried to do something about my sleeping masculinity. He hired a prostitute from the red light district in St. Louis, and locked me in a room with her for two hours. I finally broke out. Too scared to go home, I hid in the basement of a mortuary for three days. The place had what I needed most — peace and quiet to recover from the shock of my father and the whore."

Nikki mused, half-speaking to herself, "Even though it's not funny, the story always makes me laugh."

Patrick agreed. "Me too — now. He'd hired the whore when I told him I wanted to be a hairdresser, and when I came home and said I wanted to be a mortician instead, Papa said, 'I'd rather have a ghoul than a queer any day.' After that, he left me alone."

Silence filled the room. Uncomfortable, Carole asked, "Do you still wish you'd been a hairdresser?"

"Mercy, no. I have the best of both worlds. I'd go bananas in a shop with women yakking all day. This way when I do their hair, they never bitch. And one thing for sure, they always look better going out than coming in. See how nice you and Nikki look in your holiday hair?"

138

Patrick gave Carole a bear hug. "I'm not saying goodbye. Some night when this lady's working onstage peeling off her clothes, come visit me and Gil. You'll love him."

Impulsively, Carole kissed him and blurted, "I will. I'll be seeing a lot of you. I like you."

Once back in Nikki's apartment, Carole locked herself in the bathroom, turned on the makeup lamp, and scrutinized the changes. The shadow on her cheekbones created oval hollows which dramatically accentuated her eyes and mouth. The new line of her eyebrows made her eyes seem larger and set farther apart. Just like Sophia Loren's, she thought excitedly. Her hair gave her the greatest pleasure. Patrick had left its curl intact, but had shaped its unruliness so that soft curls now gracefully framed her face. She looked smaller, more delicate.

I'm really changing, thought Carole — in every way. I've never felt this pretty before. Maybe now I won't feel so plain around Nikki's friends.

They had planned to go dancing that evening at Papa Freud's. But when Carole joined Nikki in the bedroom, she found Nikki undressed and in bed.

"What are you doing? Taking a nap?"

"No. Stand at the foot of the bed," Nikki ordered softly. "I want to look at you. You're lovely."

Carole obeyed. She stood proudly before Nikki, very much aware of Nikki's pleasure in watching her.

"Now, undress slowly — one piece at a time."

"Nikki, are you going to get weird?"

"I'm going to have a good time. Do what I say," Nikki urged her.

Carole sighed. "All he did was fix my face, Nikki. The rest of me is still the same."

"Start with your sweater, then work on down."

Carole complied, self-conscious and slightly afraid. Nikki's dominant manner was new to her. She felt Nikki's eyes scan her body. Embarrassed, she hurriedly took off her bra and pants, then reached for the covers to hide herself.

Nikki held down the covers with her hand.

"Let me get in there with you." Again Carole tried to pull the covers back.

"No. I want you to circle around the bed so I can see all of you." Nikki's voice was firm. "Just do it once, then come back and sit here beside me."

"Nikki, I don't think I can do it right now," Carole said flatly. "I can't turn on just like that."

Nikki propped herself up on the pillows. Her blue eyes pleaded.

Carole snatched a pillow. Using it as a cover she walked around the bed, then sat down next to Nikki. She held the pillow on her lap while Nikki studied her face, and then dropped her gaze to Carole's breasts. Carefully, she removed the pillow from Carole's lap, exposing her fully, and once again continued to stare at the contours of Carole's body.

Her entire body warmed. She felt Nikki's eyes drift with excruciating slowness from one part of her body to another, feeling her gaze on her breasts, then a single breast, then a nipple, moving to her face, her mouth, her eyes, and finally between her legs. Helpless, Carole's body responded of its own volition wherever Nikki chose to look. The longer Nikki's stare covered her, the hotter her body became.

Seeking relief, Carole tried to make eye contact with Nikki, but Nikki refused. Slowly, with an index finger, she started massaging one of Carole's nipples. Carole felt her entire body ignite, pulsate, then in flood, submit.

Involuntarily, Carole's legs opened, but instead of entering her, Nikki softly whispered, "Stand," and when Carole did, Nikki got out of bed and spread Carole's legs farther apart, then knelt before her inhaling her scent. Nikki's tongue barely touched Carole before she arched as waves of painful ecstasy surged through her. She collapsed into Nikki's arms.

Nikki clung to her tightly. "Now you can put on all the clothes you want."

"Jesus, Nikki. What did you do? I've never felt so possessed." Carole worked to steady her breath.

Nikki drew them both back into bed and pulled the covers up. "Loving you brings me such pleasure."

"I'm glad you said that, but now I'm worried. How much of what you just did is because Patrick redesigned me?"

"None of it. He didn't give you anything that wasn't already there. But you had to like looking at yourself without feeling self-conscious before you would let me enjoy you. In a way you became a stripper today." Nikki added playfully, "I love being your audience."

Later that evening at Papa Freud's, Carole marveled at the difference in the way she felt this night as compared to that first date. She was proud of being there, proud of dancing and nestling close to Nikki. She not only belonged to Nikki, she felt they belonged at Papa Freud's, together. Looking around the club, Carole sought some of the women she had met only a few weeks before. None were present; she was robbed of the pleasure of showing off to Nikki's friends.

Once again the antics of Cretia, the black singer, titillated her. Singling out two young men sitting at the piano bar, she asked, "Didn't I sanctify your marriage?" When they didn't answer, she pointed to one of them and scolded, "You were a virgin . . ." To the audience she confided lustily, "A virgin's someone who's never had it in the . . ." Fast, thundering arpeggios masked the last word.

Her public laughed and some applauded, but Nikki quickly stopped Carole from clapping. "Don't encourage her, sweetheart. She's exploiting us."

The evening had all the smoothness and pleasure lacking in her first visit. Nikki had never been so attentive, amorous, caring. And if the audience had once upon a time appeared weird or bizarre, on this visit Carole saw only glamour.

CHAPTER SIXTEEN

Several weeks later, Carole, deeply depressed, waited for Nikki to return from her brunch with Janice. She heard the key in the door but remained on the couch — refusing to welcome her home.

"Why so sad?" asked Nikki in concern. "Why are you crying?"

Carole wiped away the tears that had gathered in the corners of her eyes. "I went over to Donna's today to pick up my Photo Four portfolio. It's seventy percent of my grade."

Nikki threw her purse down on the couch and sat close to her. She offered her arms, but Carole ignored them. Nikki asked, "May I see why you're so upset?" She reached over to untie the strings.

Carole snapped bitterly, "Don't even bother looking through the pictures. Read the yellow evaluation sheet."

Nikki read in silence, dropped the paper, and removed the pictures. "She can't be talking about your work." She spread the mounted photographs on the carpet. She studied them carefully. "They're beautiful. And this one is my favorite."

She picked up the photo of a musician playing his bass fiddle, as entwined with it as a lover, his bow caressing the strings, his eyes shut — his head bent next to the instrument.

Carole jerked the picture out of Nikki's hands. "You don't know what you're talking about. Dr. Eisenstein is right. They're stale, flat, and lack point of view." Carole threw the bassist on the carpet.

Nikki stood up angrily. "Don't be such a child! Maybe I don't know what the assignment was, but I know these are beautiful pictures." Nikki raised her voice. "Stop pouting and contest the grade."

Carole shook her head in defeat. "I'm up shit creek. I got a D in a core course. I didn't shoot any of those pictures for her class. They're all from my negative file." In a barely audible voice she added, "Some of them aren't even mine."

Shocked disbelief crossed Nikki's face. "Why?"

"Because of you!" Carole jumped up and shouted in rage, "Because I needed to be with you night and day — every minute, every moment. Haven't you noticed?"

144

Nikki, hands on her hips, said, "I'm noticing that you're trying to hang me with your irresponsibility." Her voice was cool and even. "I've done my work and assumed you were doing the same. I'm not going to wear a hairshirt because you got a D. Instead of feeling sorry for yourself, talk to Dr. Eisenstein and get her to give you an Incomplete in the course. Then make it up during the summer."

The sheer truth of Nikki's words snapped Carole out of her self-pity. She took Nikki's hand in hers and returned to the couch. "I'm too ashamed to face Dr. Eisenstein. She once told me that I had an intuitive eye for a story."

"She's right. These pictures show that."

"You don't understand. I was supposed to walk the streets to find a common theme — an aspect of humanity both particular and universal. It had to have a point of view. Instead I turned in a hodge-podge of shots hoping Eisenstein would read something into it that wasn't there."

"Well, at least you're honest," Nikki said, "but you need to take action. If worse comes to worst, tell your teacher the truth." She winked playfully.

Carole laughed loudly. "You've got to be kidding." She looked at Nikki. "You're not kidding, are you?" She would be mortified to stand before Dr. Eisenstein and disclose involvement with a lover.

"What have you got to lose?" Nikki cuddled her. "If you want," she whispered, "I'll go with you and swear it's true."

Carole said submissively, "I'll go Monday — but don't come with me . . . please."

A loud pounding on Nikki's front door made them both jump. "Who is it?" Nikki called, alarmed.

"It's Torchy. Let me in."

Carole groaned. Nikki opened the door.

Carole scarcely recognized Torchy without her stage makeup. Pale, wearing only a little rouge and lipstick, she looked like any attractive yet ordinary woman on a Saturday morning. She was dressed in jeans and a peasant blouse. Her black hair fell loosely onto her shoulders.

"It wasn't easy to come here," Torchy announced.

Nikki stepped back to let her in. "I don't imagine it was. Sit down. You know Carole."

Torchy sat stiffly in a chair. To Carole she said, "Hello. I remember you." She took a deep breath. "Look, you two, I'll get it out of the way. I'm sorry. I'm talking to both of you." She rummaged through her purse and pulled out a pack of Pall Malls.

"Why are you here?" demanded Nikki.

Torchy's lighter shook as she lit her cigarette. "Because I got my ass in a sling, and the sling's unravelling. I think you know what I mean, Nikki."

"I know the club canned you. That's all I know."

Carole picked up her pictures from the floor and started to leave.

"Stay," Torchy called, "I don't care if you hear."

"This isn't any of my business." She looked at Nikki. "I'll be in the bedroom." To Torchy, "See you around."

She closed the door to the bedroom and turned on the TV. She tried concentrating on Randolph Scott making a stand with the homesteaders against the cattlemen, but bits and scraps of Torchy and Nikki's conversation invaded her retreat. Torchy's voice rose frequently, at times charged with anger then choked with sobs.

The sounds of Torchy's anguish brought back Carole's own despair of that morning when she had read Dr.

146

Eisenstein's curt note. "Unacceptable material. No originality, no effort. Assignment unfulfilled. D."

She couldn't believe she had tried to blame Nikki, not that she had let her get away with it. Nikki should have been angrier with her. But it was true. She hadn't done her work because she had wanted only to be with Nikki. I've got to get myself together, Carole resolved.

After what seemed hours, Nikki came into the bedroom. She looked drained. She lay down on the bed next to Carole, but apart from her.

"Was it real heavy?" asked Carole, taking Nikki's hand.

Nikki gently slipped her hand out of Carole's. "It's not you, sweetheart. I have to sort things out. Do you mind if we're quiet for a while?"

"No, I'll turn off the TV."

"TV doesn't bother me," said Nikki, and closed her eyes.

Not long afterward, Carole heard the heavy, steady breathing that signaled Nikki was asleep. It was hours later, almost dusk before she woke.

"Feeling better?" Carole asked.

"Sorry. Torchy was too much."

"Couldn't you just ask her to leave? Did she want you to get her job back?" asked Carole sarcastically. "She's got a lot of nerve, after what she did to you and me."

"There's more to it than that," said Nikki ruefully. "She wants me to get her *any* job. Bert's blacklisted her and she wants me and Janice to go see him."

"Blacklisted? How can he do that?"

"He just can," stated Nikki.

Carole sat up in bed, her eyes dancing with excitement. She faced Nikki. "Oh, my God! He's a gangster, isn't he? If he can blacklist her, then he must be a gangster. I saw *The Godfather.*"

Nikki laughed. "I'll only say he's very influential in the nightclub business."

Carole jumped off the bed. "Come on, tell me. What's going on?"

"Slow down. Bert probably told his friends that Torchy has drinking problems and she's too unstable to work anymore. They'd believe him. And truthfully, he's not wrong," she conceded.

"So why doesn't she do something else?"

"She's been a strip all her life. She's been to manicure school, bartender school, but she always comes back. That's all she knows. I loaned her some money. She's flat broke."

"That's hard to believe," said Carole. "There's other jobs. She must have known she couldn't be a stripper forever. Isn't she about your age?"

Nikki smiled wryly. "Careful, cookie."

"I wasn't being rude," said Carole. "You know what I mean. You said you're going to college because it's a bail-out profession. Why didn't she look ahead?"

"Torchy had a big nest egg. Then she married Dan, a customer who was absolutely bonkers over her. He wasn't content just sleeping with her. He sent her cards, flowers, the whole deal. He wanted marriage. Torchy was flattered." Nikki added cynically, "I warned her."

"Not to get married?"

"Not to believe him. I've seen it happen so many times. These guys come in and fall in love with all the glamour. Then they marry strips, and want to turn them into plain Janes. Before you know it, they can't get it up. Soon they're out chasing around again."

"I wouldn't call Torchy a plain Jane," Carole said.

"She's settled down a lot. He wouldn't let her wear makeup at home. He made her buy ordinary clothes. Before she married him, she used to look pretty spiffy on and off stage. Once he caged her, he never took her out. Then one night Torchy went home early and caught him in the sack with another strip."

"Was that why she was so crazy that night?"

"Partly. The final blow was that he took off with everything she had."

"That's one of the worst stories I've ever heard in my life. Can't she have him arrested? How much money did she have?"

"Torchy's dream was to buy a small motel in Arizona and retire. Three years — she was that close to getting what she wanted. She can't find him. It was a joint account. There's nothing she can do."

"Are you going to see Bert?" asked Carole.

Nikki sighed tiredly. "I'm afraid so."

A cold fear gripped Carole as she saw Nikki in worried deliberation. She asked urgently, "Why is his revenge so extreme? And what if I displease him? Or you do?"

"We're in no danger," Nikki assured her. "Torchy and Bert go *way* back. She's got a big mouth and went too far." Nikki's face brightened. "I know — I'll take Janice with me! He listens to her. She can convince anyone of anything. I'll go over to her house tonight. Want to come?"

"To meet Janice? Finally?"

Nikki's gloom was gone. "Janice and June. I promise you'll like them. And I know you'll love Janice."

CHAPTER SEVENTEEN

Later that evening, Carole and Nikki sat around a huge square wooden coffee table in Janice and June's cozy living room. The walnut-paneled walls were decorated with blowups of female actresses — Hepburn, Garbo, Dietrich, Lombard, Stanwyck.

Carole liked Janice, despite Janice's candid inspection of her. She was drawn to her clear green eyes, which seemed tired with the burden of knowing. They were old, wise eyes that rarely changed expression.

When Janice moved, something about the slow graceful way she carried herself reminded Carole of Nikki. She now understood many of Nikki's mannerisms. Janice is more like Nikki than Nikki herself, thought Carole. Janice is the original.

Both Janice and Nikki spoke with as few words as possible. Both stared intently when listening. Both had a shy, reserved smile that made the recipient feel chosen.

Janice agreed to intervene on Torchy's behalf with Bert. "He's not going to like us siding with Torchy," she drawled. "But if she doesn't get some kind of stripping job soon, she'll be hitting the streets. He can get her a gig in a club out of town."

Nikki agreed. "At least in a club she can choose her johns."

The casual way that Janice and Nikki discussed prostitution shocked Carole. The strikingly handsome ash blonde in an emerald green silk smock leisurely conferring with a petite redhead in a teal blue cotton pant suit — they could have been corporate wives discussing their husbands' careers; instead they were lesbians plotting the safest way for a friend to combine stripping with hooking. And one of them, Carole thought, is my girlfriend. She shook her head in disbelief and looked away.

June however, seemed quite comfortable with the blatant dissection of Torchy's problems. A small-framed platinum blonde with dark eyes that moved rapidly from person to person, she had a warm easy laugh. Carole was grateful that when they were introduced June had not scrutinized her as closely as Janice had.

Janice had clasped her hand affectionately. "At last we're allowed to meet," Janice had said. Carole had felt the older woman's eyes slowly assess her face, body, clothing. Carole had looked helplessly at Nikki and received a reassuring wink.

June was an excellent hostess. Even though Carole and Nikki showed up unannounced, June instantly served a platter of cheese, crackers, fruit, and a carafe of dry white wine.

"Well, now that Torchy's settled, let's talk about you," Janice said to Carole. "How do you like your new lifestyle?" The question, phrased in her soft Southern accent, seemed especially disconcerting.

"Why are you asking her that?" June asked, irritated.

"It's something I want to know," Janice explained calmly. "You know I like to hear about people coming out. We're getting so damn old, we never hear any new stories."

Carole looked to Nikki for assistance.

"Make her swap stories, honey," Nikki said to Carole. "Let her tell you how it was in the old days when she was a stripper in Calumet City — Sin City."

Carole said eagerly, "That sounds like a good trade. I'm very happy with Nikki." She took a sip of her wine. "Your turn."

Janice leaned toward her. "Think you'll ever want to sleep with men again?"

"Truthfully, I've never thought about it."

Janice moved even closer to Carole. "Well, think about it. You're twenty-two, right? Is Nikki the only one you'll ever sleep with? Don't you wonder if the next one'll be male or female?"

Carole suddenly felt nervous. "Who can plan in advance? I can't." She looked at each of them. "Could any of you after your first experience?"

"Leave me out of this," June said.

"I could," said Janice. "I like to think Nikki could too."

Carole felt a twinge of jealousy and turned to Nikki, who leaned back in her chair, apparently amused at the interplay between her past and current lovers.

Carole leaned toward Janice. Their faces barely two inches apart, she said with conviction, "I cross one bridge at a time."

Janice laughed softly. "You're very attractive, Carole." She turned to Nikki. "Actually, you're both good to look at." She held them in her gaze for a few moments. "My money says you'll go a long way together."

Something about Janice's voice made Carole believe her. The thought of her and Nikki's lives being united for a long time made Carole both happy and anxious. Until now, her primary goal had been to secure Nikki's love. She had never before envisioned a lifetime with anyone. She filed away these thoughts for another time, reiterating to herself: I cross one bridge at a time.

"Okay Janice," Carole challenged, "tell me about Sin City."

"Girlfriends were harder to get in the fifties," Janice reminisced. "We'd yell at them from our second story window and invite them up."

"And they'd go?" Carole asked incredulously.

"Sometimes. Our best line was . . ." Janice made her accent especially thick, "Do yawl wanna come up and listen to our Sophie Tucker records?"

Carole burst out laughing. "What would you do once they got there?"

"Offer them drinks. Dance a little. Listen to Sophie Tucker."

"Is that all?"

June turned to Janice. "You forgot to tell her that you and your friends were in drag."

Carole giggled. "I don't believe it. You mean you were dressed like men? How old were you?"

Janice looked at Carole teasingly. "About your age. But we had to be careful. The word around town was, we had to wear three pieces of feminine clothing. We could get busted for cross-dressing."

"That doesn't sound legal," Carole argued. "There had to be more to it. Weren't there any gay clubs then?"

Janice sliced some cheese. "We had them, but the cops could come in at any time and arrest us if we were touching. I was a stripper and so were my friends, so the cops were easier on us. The bulldykes had it the roughest."

"Why?" asked Carole. "Were they that strange?"

Nikki explained, "In a way they were. Some dressed like men. They taped down their breasts and wore boxer shorts, men's socks, shoes —" She broke off. "Their whole attire was masculine. They were persecuted horribly. Whatever freedom we enjoy today comes from them and their refusal to be closeted. They took all the brutality."

"I never realized," Carole murmured.

June refilled everyone's glass. She said, "Parents could have their gay daughters arrested and thrown into a mental ward. It happened to a friend of ours. She was living with her lover when the police came and took her. The parents said she was mentally unstable."

A sick feeling came over Carole. How could she possibly tell her Jewish parents about her new lifestyle?

"You haven't told your parents, have you?" Janice asked, almost tenderly. Her green eyes were fastened acutely on Carole.

"I've been too involved to think of them," Carole said. She felt her throat tighten.

"Look at it from their point of view." Janice moved closer to her and rested a hand on her shoulder. "This is a hard life. You'll always be an outsider. Your folks may want your happiness, but the fact is, when you tell them you're gay they'll feel ashamed."

Big tears rolled down Carole's cheeks. In the quiet room, Janice wrapped her arms about her. She felt solace in the strength of Janice's embrace. The room remained quiet until she pulled herself together.

Nikki moved to the other side of Carole. She said firmly. "Gay life is *not* tragic — I don't see it that way."

June said, "I agree. We have our own freedoms — as long as we stay with our own kind. Janice started earlier than most of us. She remembers how it was."

Janice released Carole and picked up a glass of wine. "That's right. I was fifteen and lived in a small Louisiana town. I knew I didn't fit in, so I stole a bike and rode six hours till I caught up with the circus and got my first job. I was one of eighty girls up in the webbing — I made my living being twirled on a rope a hundred feet above the crowd. It was rough, but worth it." Janice took a deep drag on her cigarette. "I went with the circus to Baltimore and East St. Louis where I learned to strip. Next came Chicago and Calumet City."

For the rest of the evening Janice held court. Carole sat back, charmed by Janice's storytelling, spellbound by lusty, funny tales about gay life back in the fifties.

At home, Carole was non-communicative. She was trying to retain the intimacy of the evening and the magic of Janice.

155

Nikki said, "Tomorrow would be a good day for you to go and see Dr. Eisenstein about changing your grade to an Incomplete."

"I don't feel like talking about it," Carole said curtly.

"Why do I get the feeling that Janice is still in your head?"

Wistfully, Carole said, "My life is so boring compared to hers. How can I consider myself an artist when I've seen so little?"

Nikki took Carole by the hand and led her toward the bedroom. "The enchantress has done it again. Those same tales captivated me too, years ago. Janice can still weave a spell."

"Do you still love her?" Carole asked. "I'm not jealous. I can see why you would. She's so powerful — yet gentle. I can't figure out why you're still not together. You're prettier than June."

Nikki said tiredly, "We talked about this before. No, I'm not in love with Janice. I love her dearly, but I'm in love with you and right now you seem far away." She undressed herself and then Carole. "Put on your night shirt. Let's get to bed."

"But now I'm really interested," Carole insisted. "How did Janice tell you she was leaving you?"

"We were in Singapore. Then she flew back home to look for what she called a real job. Then she called me long distance." Nikki pulled back the covers and motioned Carole into bed.

"Tell me exactly what she said."

Nikki assumed a Southern drawl and sarcastically mimicked, "Tahm for us to tally up our bills. Ah met someone else."

Carole snuggled close to her. "She didn't say it that way. That sounds mean. I can't imagine Janice being mean."

"Janice isn't mean. She's blunt." Nikki placed her hand between Carole's legs. "Do stories about the good old days always turn you on this way?"

Surprised at her wetness, Carole admitted, "I guess they do."

She turned hungrily to Nikki seeking quick gratification. Her body throbbed with desire. She opened her legs and pleaded, "Make love to me."

Nikki slowly caressed Carole's breasts, but went no further. Her mouth lingered over Carole's thighs.

Tormented by Nikki's reticence, Carole took hold of Nikki's head and pleaded, "Now, Nikki!"

Abruptly Nikki stopped and pulled away from Carole. Carole looked down, confused. "What —"

Nikki took the sheet and blotted Carole's passion. Paralyzed, Carole felt like a child being cleansed.

"There," said Nikki in a low forceful voice. "Now I can love you. Get wet again, Carole. Get wet for me only."

Hypnotized by Nikki's imperious tone, Carole surrendered. Nikki alternated between aggression and tenderness, prolonging her lovemaking, maintaining Carole on the edge of fulfillment. Carole cried for her to finish. With her tongue, Nikki brought her to a painful ecstatic release.

Grateful, Carole opened her arms and embraced Nikki. "It's you. It's you. It will always be you."

CHAPTER EIGHTEEN

All morning Carole had worked reorganizing her darkroom, determined to restore Dr. Eisenstein's faith in her as a photographer.

Dressed in an elegant aqua silk suit, Nikki entered unannounced and stretched out on Carole's bed, her red hair decorating the pillow. "Janice and I were at Bert's talking to him about Torchy." She lazily kicked off her shoes. "I've decided to strip in Quebec this summer. I'm taking you with me."

"Quebec?" Carole asked, alarmed. "Did you forget I have to make up the Incomplete for Eisenstein this summer? My folks won't support my traveling around Canada with a — a —" She saw Nikki's expression. "You know what I mean," she added apologetically.

"It won't cost your parents a cent. I'll pay for everything. I've been thinking, why do you need this apartment? You're always at my place." Nikki smiled. "I like that." She added, "Have you ever thought of giving up this place?"

Carole held up her hands. "Stop. You're going too fast. Start from the beginning. What happened with Torchy?"

"We got her a job in Vegas. That's the most Bert would allow. She'll have to toe the line — obey house rules — that means putting out whether she wants to or not." Nikki's voice was tinged with sadness. "It's a hard way to make money, but she'll do it, she's desperate. Carole, let me get to the good news."

"Is this the part where I go to Quebec or where I give up my apartment?"

Nikki sat up. Her face brightened. "Bert offered me a fantastic deal for the summer. I've thought it through. I want you to come with me." She looked at Carole meaningfully. "Let your apartment go — move into my place."

The earnestness in Nikki's face and voice kindled Carole's love. She had never heard such vehemence from Nikki. A warm flush coursed through her as she savored the sweet strength of the bond she felt for her lover.

She forced herself to look away. The tenderness of the moment faded as her eyes surveyed her apartment, the first home she had made, that she had so proudly come to

159

view as a symbol of her self. Nearly suffocated by a whirlwind of emotions, she asked, "Will I end up changing *all* my life for you?"

Nikki motioned Carole to her, wrapped her arms tightly around her waist and rocked her gently. In the silence Carole became conscious of herself and Nikki breathing in the same cadence.

Nikki spoke softly. "Carole, you're not changing all your life for me. We're just going away for the summer. Keep this place, if you feel you need to. I was out of line asking you to give it up."

"I can't give it up. It's too important." Carole felt her tenseness ease. "Tell me about Quebec, but don't stop holding me."

Nikki gave her a squeeze and kissed her forehead. "Bert can get me a ten week contract in Quebec. I'd net seven hundred a week, tax free, plus room and board. I'd be the only headliner in each club." Nikki stopped and took a deep breath. "It's the chance of a lifetime." Her voice rose with excitement. "There's over a hundred strips for every job."

Carole remembered the conversation about Torchy stripping and hooking. "What do you have to do for seven hundred dollars a week?" she probed.

Nikki pulled away. "I don't hook, if that's what you're implying. You know goddamn well I've never hooked."

"Sorry, the high salary made me suspicious. Are you sure?"

Nikki took hold of Carole's hand. "The pay is good because I'll be working clubs in remote areas. Miners and mill workers go there and blow their paychecks." Her face glowed as she continued. "It's my chance to quit stripping for good. I won't have to work while I'm in graduate school. Carole, I need you with me. Quebec is rough." She added quickly, "But I can take care of us."

Carole lowered her head. "I don't feel comfortable accepting your money."

"Consider it a salary," Nikki said lightly. "I won't go without you."

She resisted. "Nik, I want to help you, but I've got a timetable of my own."

"I figured that out already. You can work on your project while we're there. Carole, wait until you see the forests, the mountains, the St. Laurence River." Nikki pointed to the wall of ghetto portraits. "And if it's subject matter you're after, I hear the living conditions of the Indians in Northern Quebec are terribly harsh. That should give you plenty to work with."

Carole deliberated. "I've shot enough nature in Oregon to last me a lifetime. The Indians would be interesting."

Nikki stressed, "Whether I go or not depends on you. I won't go on the road alone anymore. It's too lonely." She leaned over and put on her shoes.

"Don't go, Nikki. I can't give you an answer yet. Let me think about it. I have to call home."

"Why? You're an adult. You're always talking about wanting to go out and experience the world. Now's your chance. I need to know soon. Contracts have to be signed tomorrow." Without another word, she left.

Carole breathed deeply, seeking relief from her absence. She could hear Nikki's footsteps, and with every step, she grew lonelier, more afraid. The car door slammed; the motor turned; there was the sound of Nikki's car driving away. She looked at her watch. Half an hour. It had taken Nikki barely half an hour to turn her life upside down.

She scanned her apartment. All that really mattered was the darkroom. Even her wall of pictures seemed naive, stale — now.

I don't know where she's leading me. Why am I letting her do this? My love should have leveled off by now. I'm more caught up with her than ever.

But, she asked me to live with her. She asked me — finally.

She let herself collapse on the bed. The pain of indecision gnawed at her. In what seemed a lifetime ago, she had run to Nikki for friendship, for love. In the pursuit, she had lost part of herself — her contact with the solid world she knew.

How did I get from there to here? she wondered. Nikki had replaced every passion. Why did she feel so alien in her own place? She craved someone to talk to. Patrick.

"What has happened to my Carole? You look like one of the hags the county asks us to fix up."

"I feel worse. I need to talk to you."

He ushered her in with a flourish. "Auntie Patrick's an expert on advice to the lovelorn."

"Oh, Patrick, I wish it were that simple." She sighed and told him about Quebec. "I feel I'm losing control of my life."

Patrick became serious, business-like. "You didn't lose control. Why should gay commitments be different? Someone always compromises in a relationship. If you're scared of going, don't go. There's no legal contract holding you together. You two don't even have joint debts to bind you."

"But what if she leaves me? What if she finds someone else? I can't risk losing her. Would you risk losing Gil?"

162

"No. We've been together fifteen years and seen the heights and the pits."

"Has it been worth it?"

"Yes . . ." He paused. "But what else can I say? I've thrown everything I have into this marriage. Once though," he reminisced sadly, "I nearly sent the bitch packing when he thought he was in love with someone else."

"What did you do?"

"Well, after I broke everything in the house, including the dining room table, and after he cut my lip with a butch right cross, we made up and ran off to Queen City for a week. We each went trashin' every night, got it out of our system, then came home with our prostates aching. Bought new stuff for the house and got deeper in debt."

Carole wrinkled her nose. "That's hardly a happy ending, Patrick."

He arched his eyebrows. "Well dearie, you know the saying. Different strokes for us old goats."

Carole laughed at his theatrics. Then she remembered that Nikki had to sign the contracts the next day. "Come to think of it, there's nothing to hold me in L.A. but Nikki. I'm with her all the time. I'm beginning to feel like a stranger in my own place. The darkroom is filled with unprinted negatives I used to think were so important. Shit!" Carole shouted. "I don't even know how gay I am or if I want to stay that way!"

Patrick leaned back in his chair and cast an exaggerated sidelong glance at her. "With or without Nikki, I think it's too late. You've drunk of the absinthe. There's a reason why that drink was banned."

Worried, she said, "You don't mean I can't ever be straight again?"

Patrick's demeanor changed. He studied Carole for a long time. He took her hands in his and asked gently, "Would you want to be?"

Journal Entry — June 15, 1973

It wasn't until Nikki asked me to give up my apartment and live with her that I realized I wasn't really living with her. I was only staying with her. I thought I'd made a commitment to her. If I did, then why am I so afraid of going with her to Quebec?

Where's the photo journalist in me? Here I am hesitating at the chance to see something new. NEW. Maybe that's the trouble. I don't think I can handle any more new things in my life.

Why am I kidding myself? I know I won't let her go without me. I can't be without her.

CHAPTER NINETEEN

Carole helped Nikki prepare costumes, props, and music for the road. Long distance phone calls from Quebec would often wake them during the night as details over itinerary, salary, and contract conditions were sorted, re-negotiated.

Major complications arose when Nikki was notified by a midnight phone call that her acts had to be five minutes longer and that one of them had to be a "strong act."

"Do you know what that means?" Nikki asked, her face flushed with anger. "They want me to spread my legs wide open in front of everyone. That's what it means!"

Together they went to see Bert.

Hands trembling, Nikki pleaded, "I know you can amend the contract."

"Impossible," Bert said. "Not if you want the salary. Too many strips will show everything for that kind of money." He said with finality, "If you accept the contract, you have to do it, especially if it's with my endorsement. Talk to Janice. She'll help you."

Once out of the office, Nikki turned to Carole and whispered rebelliously, "I'll sign the contract — but when I'm on stage, I'll make sure they don't get a whole look."

Relieved, Carole asked, "You mean you're not going to do it?"

"If I show anything, it'll be with a heavy pussy toupee."

Carole giggled uncontrollably. "Is there really such a thing?"

Nikki joined the laughter. "In all colors and sizes!"

In front of Donato's office on Beverly Drive, Nikki took Carole in her arms and kissed her fully, lingeringly on the lips. Passing cars honked at them. Nikki and Carole smiled, waved. Nikki took a bow.

Three days before departure, Nikki had a recording studio extend her music the necessary five minutes. She picked up her costumes from the cleaners. She re-stocked her stage makeup and purchased her secondary wardrobe.

As she unpacked a matching forest green skirt and sweater from a Bullock's box, she explained to Carole, "I'll have to look good whether on stage or not.

166

Everybody sizes up the new girl in town." She added reassuringly, "You can wear what you want."

Nikki's tone became stern, preachy. "We've got to be careful how we act. It's a well-traveled circuit. If we do something wrong, the news will get to the next club before we do. I'd hate to disappoint Bert . . ." Nikki trailed off.

Carole snapped a close-up shot of her. All morning she had been photographing her racing around the costume-strewn living room fitting her clothing into two large trunks.

Nikki had objected sharply to Carole's constant picture-taking.

"Nik, pretend I'm not here. I want a memory of this forever." Again, Carole aimed the camera at Nikki. "I want to make a photo essay of this trip. I'm titling it, *High Contrast*. I'm trying to show how much clothing you have to wear just to end up naked onstage." Carole took another picture. "I think I could make it kind of funny."

Nikki blocked the lens with her hand. "You're getting on my nerves," she said and pushed the camera away.

Carole raised the Nikon above her head. "Don't touch my camera like that," she barked. She stormed into the kitchen.

Nikki's brusque handling of her equipment angered and hurt her. Again she wondered if the trip was a mistake. They'd never traveled together, how would they get along? She recalled the quarrel-filled family vacations when her father would threaten to take them back home.

Nikki skulked into the kitchen. They sat in silence, avoided contact. "Look," Carole ventured cautiously, "are you sure you still want me to go? I'd understand if you changed your mind. This fighting isn't worth it."

"It's not you." Nikki ran both hands through her hair in exasperation. "It's my acts! I haven't done what Bert

167

ordered. I can't do a hard act! I don't have a clue how to fake it."

"Wasn't Janice supposed to help?"

Nikki glanced at her watch. She slammed her fist on the table. "That bitch was due over an hour ago. How can she be late when she knows I need her?"

Shocked, Carole asked, "Why are you so mad? I've never seen you this way." Seeking to divert Nikki's anger, she asked, "Was Janice as good a dancer as you?"

"Shit, I don't know," Nikki said impatiently. "Who cares?"

"I want to know," Carole insisted. She toyed with Nikki's hair. "Tell me."

Nikki calmed down. "We use two different styles. I learned the best of my craft in Paris. Janice knows more specialty and novelty stuff. But then I've never had to work a place as rough as Calumet City," she added. "That hell hole forced Janice to pick up a lot of techniques."

"Do you think she'd mind if I took pictures?"

Nikki glowered. "Carole, if you're going to go ga-ga all over Janice the way you did the other night, leave."

Stunned, Carole rose. "Look Nik, I'm not interested in Janice. She's just a far-out lady. But if you want, I'll go." She hesitated by the door.

"Stay," Nikki murmured. She reached out. "I'm scared."

The moment Janice walked in, Nikki's reserve broke, as if she had been holding herself together until help arrived. Carole had never seen her so volatile, uncooperative, stubborn. Put off by her, Carole remained silent letting Janice take the brunt of Nikki's tension.

168

"Let me see what you've worked out so far," Janice said.

"I've done nothing — except wait for you," Nikki said sarcastically.

Janice said, "Good. You don't have anything to unlearn. Get in costume."

Nikki shook her head. "No, I don't want to get them sweaty."

"Well, at least put on some makeup. You look like hell."

"Live with it," Nikki snarled. "I don't want to have to clean my face again. It's too hot."

She balked at Janice's request to strip totally; instead, she danced in leotards and heels. "I'm not going to spread my legs here or anywhere else. I can't. I can't!" She burst into tears.

Carole hurried to comfort her. Nikki leaned against her and cried.

Janice stood with her arms crossed. "When you're finished bawling, I'll show you how to do it. Carole sugar, get a dining room chair, please."

Janice said, as she placed herself on the chair, "Okay, you two sit in front of me and watch. It's all in the knees. You take off the G-string sitting down. At the same time, you flip your hair forward so they can't see your crotch. Then, you toss the string to the front row." Janice demonstrated the moves several times.

As Nikki watched, she counted the beats with her hand.

Janice continued, "Next, spread yourself across the chair so your feet and hair almost touch the floor. Draw your knees against your chest and twist so your legs are against the back of the chair."

169

Again Janice modeled, first in slow motion, then at normal speed. "Keep your legs pointed up, but drop your head back and use your hair as a prop. Play with your hair slowly. Get sexy, child. You know how to do that. Scissor your legs at the same time, or open them and stroke the inside of your thighs. Remember, as long as your legs are in the air, you can spread 'em wide as you want and no one can see a thing. All the while, use your arms to draw someone toward you."

Janice sat up in the chair and reached for a cigarette. "That's how to do it. The legs are open. You've met your contract. No one can see a thing. It's all illusion. Do it now Nikki, to the Aznavour piece."

Carole was astounded at the ease with which Nikki followed Janice's directions. Within twenty minutes she had the routine down pat. But Janice had moved mechanically, and Nikki moved with a slow, graceful motion. The vulgarity that the promoters had demanded was implied, but veiled by her subtle sensuality.

Carole became aroused as she saw Nikki caressing her thighs and breasts. She looked at Janice for evidence of a similar reaction. She saw none. When Nikki completed her act without a single hitch, Carole and Janice applauded enthusiastically.

Dripping with perspiration, Nikki kissed Janice on the forehead. "Thank you. You're wonderful! I was ready to cancel everything. Have a drink while I take a shower. Call June and we'll all go out to dinner. My treat." Without waiting for an answer, she disappeared.

Carole shook her head in disbelief. "She's back to her old self again. I've never seen Nikki the way she was this morning. It scared me."

"She panics when the road's not clear. It usually doesn't last long," Janice said calmly, knowingly. She smiled as if amused. "A few minutes ago she treated me like I was a monster. Now she's telling me I'm wonderful."

"She's right," said Carole. "You really did save her ass. She has so much faith in you. I'm jealous because I couldn't help her. Bert was sure you could."

Janice seemed pleased to hear of Bert's faith in her. "Nice to know he remembers. Is there any white wine?"

Carole returned from the kitchen with three glasses, thinking that Janice looked particularly pretty today. How strange that out of all Nikki's friends, the one she liked the most was her former lover. "Have you seen Nikki like this a lot?" She felt as if she were prying.

"I've dried a few of her tears," Janice said noncommittally. She poured wine into two glasses. "Also swept up broken glass after some of her tantrums." Janice's green eyes narrowed. "How prepared are you for this trip, kid?"

"You can sound so tough sometimes," Carole laughed. "If it wasn't for your Southern accent, I'd swear you were Humphrey Bogart or Jimmy Cagney."

Janice pressed. "Answer the question."

Carole shrugged. "I don't know. Nikki already warned me it's going to be rough — but you're obviously trying to tell me something else." Carole's stomach tightened.

Janice took her time sipping her wine, lighting a cigarette. "It's a killer. You're always on the move — always tired. Working the road isn't like playing a club. You're in strange places and at the mercy of the locals. They know the stripper can't protect herself. She's an

171

out-of-towner and they're out to get every piece of her they can. The strain — it gets to you."

Janice pointed to the bedroom. "*She* thinks she's safe with what I taught her. Believe me, Nikki will not be the same dancer we just saw in this living room. She's forgotten how hungry men get in the wilds. Savages."

Exasperated, Carole asked, "So what's the big word of advice, Janice? Give me the bottom line."

"Patience."

"Is that what you ran out of when you two broke up?" Carole probed.

Janice took a deep drag of her cigarette. She gave Carole a long lingering look. "Are you pressing for a nitty-gritty talk, Carole?"

She felt nervous. "I always wondered what happened between you two. Do you mind talking about it?"

"Not really. I ran out of patience — because I was afraid. I could see Nikki's career taking off. I was standing still — drifting backwards — know what I mean? I'd started as her teacher and lover and ended up her assistant and traveling companion."

"That would be hard to take," Carole conceded. "I worry about losing my own self to Nikki. If that happened, it would kill our relationship too."

"It killed ours. Those suitors of hers didn't help either."

"Suitors?" Carole shook her head. "That's weird — Nikki's always spoken of her commitment to you. I was under the impression you dumped her for June."

"Not exactly true. I left Nikki before I met June. When I met June, my ego was starved. Nikki did that to me." Janice looked at Carole. "June healed me."

Janice's words refueled her fears about the future. To make matters worse, Janice had brought up a new issue.

172

"Should I worry about suitors?" Carole asked. She felt unable to relieve her anxiety.

Janice chuckled. "Not about Nikki and men, or women either. Nikki's loyal to the person she's with. She doesn't sleep around. But she's flattered real easy, at least she was years ago. She got gifts from hangers-on — clothes, flowers, jewelry. She was the darling of the club owners. The other strips were after her too."

Janice's voice lowered. Her eyes looked past Carole as if seeing into the past. "Day or night, we were never alone. No privacy — no closeness . . ."

"You're bumming me out," Carole said with a sigh. "I thought going on the trip would make us closer."

"It might. Take what I say with a grain of salt. Nikki's changed. She's older now and you have your photography. I had nothing of my own — I gave everything to her. It's different with you two." Janice paused. "But if things get rough, hang in there. If she gets moody or weird, blame it on the road. You'll only be gone a summer."

Janice raised her glass of wine and toasted Carole. "I know you're going to make it. I'm counting on you, kid."

Carole clinked her glass to Janice's. "I'll write and let you know how close you called the shots."

Janice winked at Carole. "I hope you write because you want to stay in touch with me." She leaned over and lightly touched the back of Carole's hand.

Carole blushed. Unable to sustain Janice's steady gaze, she rose quickly. "I wonder what's keeping Nikki?"

Janice laughed loudly. "I'm harmless." She reached for another Marlboro. "Five'll get you twenty she's asleep right now."

Carole remembered the numerous times that Nikki had dozed off unexpectedly. "No bet. She falls asleep at the drop of a hat. Did she do that with you?"

173

"It's how she deals with pressure."

In the bedroom, they found Nikki fast asleep wrapped in a blue terrycloth robe.

CONTACT PRINT VII

Singapore — 1968

Nikki had been working the Golden Dragon for three months when the young, feisty emcee invited her to an after-hours tour of Singapore. "Come with me tonight. You'll see something foreigners never see," he promised.

"No, thank you," Nikki said. "I've been tired lately. Best I go home after the show."

"You haven't been tired," he chided. "You've been lonely and sad since Miss Janice left. Has she written? Is she coming back?"

Nikki laughed bitterly. "You don't miss a thing, do you? Yes, Miss Janice called. No. She's not coming back."

He persisted. "I think you need to see something more than this club. You need to stop thinking about your girlfriend. Come with me tonight."

At three a.m. he drove her in his small red sports car toward downtown. "When you leave Singapore, where will you go?" he asked.

"I open at the Crazy Horse in Paris, after the first of the year. I have a year contract."

"You're not going to get homesick?"

Nikki said ruefully, "I'm not interested in going home yet."

The emcee pulled into a dark alley lined with two story buildings.

Light spilled from the open doorways. He escorted her into a small room where people sat at a table playing cards, gambling. "We're here," he said.

"Where are we?" Nikki asked.

"Chinese death house," he announced.

"Where are we, really? I see people laughing, talking, playing cards, like in the marketplace."

"Truly, Miss Nikki. This is a death house. Those people are here to help the dying. My father died here last week."

He took her by the hand and led her to an incense-filled room that served as a temple for a monk chanting over a casket. Displayed on a table nearby were a large red paper car, pink cookies, phony money, little candies wrapped in foil.

In amazed obedience Nikki followed him down a stifling hot, dimly-lit corridor of single rooms. Within she saw bunk beds piled high against the walls, containing old, emaciated people in varying states of consciousness. She heard the moans of the sick and dying. On the walls she saw nails where people had hung what was left of their worldly possessions — shirts, belts, pants.

"This is appalling," Nikki said.

"I was very sad to bring my father here last week," he recounted with tears in his eyes. "We Chinese believe that it is bad luck for anyone to die in the home. I needed to see this again. Thank you for coming with me. Let's go for a drink."

"I surprised myself," Nikki explained to her escort in a hotel bar. "I felt detached from it all. The more I saw, the more I retreated. Perhaps it was because of the language barrier, though that doesn't make sense."

"Many would not have stayed as long as you." The emcee finished his fourth scotch and soda.

"You gave me no choice," Nikki said. She pointed to his empty glass. "Shouldn't you slow down on that?"

He proceeded to get very drunk. He rambled on about every local scandal and rumor. In a slurring stupor, he warned Nikki to beware of the Prince of Malaysia who came to Singapore, kidnapped young women and took them back to his kingdom.

Near dawn, Nikki tried to lead him back to his car. He insisted on walking without help and fell headlong into a drainage ditch. She wrestled him up out of the mud, got him into his car, and left him passed out over his steering wheel. She took a cab home.

CHAPTER TWENTY

Quebec, Canada — 1973

Nikki's first stop on the tour was Coulterville, a small mining town in the highest point of northeastern Quebec. They arrived at Montreal airport, switched from a luxurious jet to a medium-sized prop-assist aircraft, and flew to Rimouski where they were to begin the last leg of the trip.

The Rimouski airport was a little larger than a football field and lacking in all the amenities — no loudspeaker, no baggage carriers, no air-conditioning. But there was no shortage in people departing and arriving.

The weather was hot and humid. Carole and Nikki hauled their heavy luggage from one gate to the next before they were told by a tall young man drinking beer at the bar, "Go to Gate Three and get in line. We'll leave as soon as there's eight people."

Nikki looked at the distance to Gate Three. She took a deep sigh and looked fetchingly into the young man's eyes. "Isn't there anyone to carry this for us?"

He smiled knowingly. "You gals must be in show business. I've seen enough of you to know. I just moved out here from Toronto."

Nikki answered, "We're from Hollywood."

Carole felt flattered at being included. She had noticed that in this rural Canadian setting everyone openly gawked at Nikki's conspicuous glamour. She glided through them as if oblivious to their stares.

Realization crossed his face. "Dancers! You're going to Coulterville. You're the strippers!" His voice was loud and excited enough to make passers-by slow down to take an extra look.

Nikki smiled at him. "Can't *you* help us with the luggage?" she asked coyly.

The young man downed the rest of his beer and put on sunglasses. "I'll find someone. Get in line. I'll be taking off soon."

Incredulous, Carole asked, "*You're* the pilot?"

"Sure am," he grinned proudly.

"But you just had a beer." Carole pointed to the empty bottle.

"Canadian beer's the strongest and best in the world. I hope you ladies'll have a few with me. It's the only thing to drink in this weather."

Nikki put a silencing hand on Carole's shoulder and pushed her gently toward Gate Three where, tickets in hand, six male passengers waited to board.

The pilot and an assistant struggled with the weight of Nikki's two trunks. "Miss," the pilot said, trying to catch his breath, "I can't put these on board — too much weight."

"Oh course you can," Nikki said softly. "I need them to open tonight." She smiled at the pilot and the rest of the passengers.

"Lady, you don't understand," he said seriously. "There's a weight limit. I got two passengers or two trunks too many. You're the only ones with luggage."

Carole pulled Nikki to the side. "Let's leave the luggage behind for now. They can ship it tomorrow. We'll pay for an extra ticket if we have to. The club owner will understand."

"Don't say another word," Nikki whispered. She opened her purse and pulled out a pink sheet of paper and showed it to the other six passengers and the pilot. In a loud voice she announced, "This is my contract saying I will open tonight at the eleven o'clock show. It says, 'This contract is PLAY or PAY, other than an Act of God.'"

Nikki handed the contract to the pilot and gestured for him to let the others see it. One by one, the passengers read the contract and nodded to Nikki as if to say, "You're telling the truth."

Nikki looked at the passengers. She let her gaze linger on each face. She sighed deeply and with an air of helplessness said, *"Je cherche deux homines qui puissent m'aider a satisfaire les conditions de mon contract."*

The men looked at each other and then one stepped forward and said, *"Je peux vous aider Mademoiselle."*

The man next to him said, *"Moi aussi."*

Nikki firmly grasped their hands and said, *"Merci beaucoup. Je me souvienderai toujours de votre gentillese."*

The hot, bumpy, grueling six hour trip was made bearable only when Carole, Nikki, and the rest of the passengers joined the young pilot in his beer drinking.

Nikki's victory over the luggage problem had won her the respect of the travelers — especially Carole, who was bursting to praise her ingenuity. She felt foolish remembering her suggestion that they leave the luggage behind. From now on, she vowed, she would sit back and let her take charge.

She opened another beer and listened to Nikki's French renditions of life in Hollywood. The men were attentive and obviously charmed when Nikki's French vocabulary failed and she improvised with expressive hand gestures. Seven hundred miles and four stops later, the two-prop, eight-passenger plane landed on a packed-dirt airstrip.

Unaccustomed to the strength of Canadian beer, Carole's head was spinning as they deplaned in the desolate outskirts of Coulterville. The pilot and Nikki guided her to the airport building, a bungalow manned by a burly, dark, middle-aged man. He collected ten dollars from each passenger, strained as he loaded the trunks onto a battered VW van, then chauffeured them at high speed over an uneven, dusty road. Carole shut her eyes and buried her face in her hands.

"Hotel Paree," he announced as he pulled up in front of a row of one-story clapboard motel rooms.

"Gotta be kidding," Carole slurred, looking at the hotel. "I don't feel so good. Lemme out of here." She fumbled for her purse and jacket.

Nikki leaned over and slid back the van door. "You need air," she said urgently. "Give me your things."

Carole stepped onto the sidewalk, her head heavy, her mouth bitter. "I'm making a fool of myself, Nikki," she said and vomited.

Nikki turned to the chauffeur and said, *"Mon amie ne se sent pas bien."* Nikki put her arm around Carole's waist, holding her up until Carole was able to stand by herself.

The driver threw back his head and laughed. *"Elle est soule!* Good-naturedly, he carried the luggage to the office, banged on the door and bellowed, *"La danseuse est arrivee!"*

Nikki tipped him and waved goodbye as the van rattled away. A sick Carole sat on the office steps. "You'll feel better now," Nikki said. "You need something to eat."

"Don't mention food," Carole begged, holding her head. "Why did I do this?" she moaned. She saw Nikki struggle with the luggage and forced herself to stand. "Some help I am."

Several trips later, the luggage was finally in the room. Carole's head-spinning stopped as soon as she stretched out on the pale green chenille bedspread. She dozed. When she woke, she found a ham sandwich and a Coca-Cola on the night-stand.

She saw Nikki unpacking, and studied her face for resentment or anger. She saw neither. She got up. "Let me do some of that."

"How are you feeling?"

"Embarrassed — foolish — afraid you're angry with me."

Nikki draped her costumes across the chair. She took Carole's hand and led her to the bed. "I'm too jittery to be angry with you. Opening night always does this to me. Eat your sandwich. It's the best I could find around here."

Obediently, she unwrapped the sandwich. "Aren't you going to eat?"

Nikki shook her head. "I had some soup at a little café down the road. Besides, I never eat before I go on, remember?"

"What's the town like?" Carole took a sip of her Coke.

"I don't want to ruin the surprise — or should I say, lessen the shock. You'll have to see it for yourself tomorrow."

Carole looked out the window into opaque darkness. "It feels weird to be in a place and not know what it looks like. I feel blind. What time are we due at the club?"

Nikki suddenly looked uncomfortable. "They said they're sending a man for *me* at ten o'clock. They said they don't want the responsibility of taking care of two women. Things are pretty cramped over there. Apparently my dressing room is the manager's office."

"Are you saying I have to stay here — alone?" She was dumbfounded. She looked around at the room — bare walls, a small closet and bathroom. "Seven nights, *here*? They don't even have a TV. I'm not going to stay in this room. I'll go out. Walk around."

"Please don't," Nikki begged. "Honey, remember this is a mining town. Lots of men alone. They've got nothing to do at night but drink." She touched Carole's face. "I'd die if anything happened to you. We'll go out together in the morning. I promise."

Seeing the worry on Nikki's face, she dropped the issue. "You haven't forgotten about the Indians, have you? Where do they live?"

"I'll find out tonight. The café owner told me the men in town work the mines in summer, then go back home in the winter. The Indians live here year round." Nikki put her arms around her. "Don't look so depressed. I need you to keep my spirits up. I'm scared shitless about opening tonight."

She snuggled against Nikki. "I'm sorry. I was being selfish. I've got to keep telling myself it's only for a week. Right?"

"That's right," Nikki reassured her. "We're starting in the worst place of all — the wilds. From here we work our way toward Montreal. There'll be more to do in bigger towns and the men won't be as rough."

She saw how much Nikki was working to cheer her up, and felt ashamed that she had needed so much bolstering. Nikki's kind patience moved her. She resolved to make herself worthy of her faith. "Don't worry about me anymore."

"That makes me happy." Nikki pulled Carole's face close to hers. "We have to take care of each other. Home is far away and . . ."

Listening to Nikki, Carole felt a new, more tangible bond between them. She realized that they had crossed into a deeper level of love, a level of caring for and nurturing of one another, and that the give and take came from another part of the self.

Nikki was in full makeup and dressed for the first show when the bodyguard, who introduced himself as Marc, came for her at ten o'clock. She threw on a long red cape, handed him garment bags containing costumes and after-show street clothes, and blew Carole a goodbye kiss. "Don't forget to lock yourself in."

Carole rose and turned the deadbolt. Its loud click underscored her aloneness. She looked through the stack of paperback books Nikki had brought with her. Nothing tempted her. She considered writing her parents. And tell them what? That she got drunk on the plane and threw up?

She looked around for her camera equipment and decided to check it for damage. She examined her telephoto and fish-eye lenses and became disgusted with her neglect of the expensive gear. She sure didn't know how to handle love and work at the same time.

All evening she labored, meticulously cleaning, and polishing. She remembered how carefully she had researched the purchase of each item, and how she had revelled in the joy of ownership.

I'm so glad I have this. How could I have forgotten how much photography means to me? My God, I have Nikki and this, my two loves. I don't need anything else.

Absorbed in readying her equipment and planning for the project, she was shocked when Nikki banged on the door and announced, "I'm home. Open up."

She bounded into the room, costumes in hand. "Thank God, you waited up for me!" she exclaimed, out of breath, her face flushed. "I was afraid you'd be asleep and wouldn't hear me."

"Is it two o'clock already?"

"Two-thirty. What a night!" Nikki pulled off her cape and threw her clothing across the chair. "Now I know why they're paying me a thousand dollars a week to work here. I'm earning the extra three hundred."

"That bad?" Carole asked. "Start at the beginning."

Nikki's eyes glowed with excitement. "The manager's office is the size of the bed — maybe smaller." She held her nose. "Only one toilet in the whole place. When I had to use it, Marc, *my bodyguard*," Nikki said, fluttering her eyelashes in mock coquetry, "barred the door."

"Did they have toilet paper?"

"I prepared for that." Nikki opened her purse and waved a package of Kleenex. "Anyway, let me tell you — there's a white fence about a foot high around the whole stage. When I complained that the audience wouldn't be able to see my footwork, the manager actually pointed to my tits and crotch and said, " *'Thees* — not feet — ees what they here for.' "

They laughed until tears poured.

"And he was right," Nikki continued. "As soon as I took off my top, the tongue-flicking started. I've never seen so many tongues in my life." Clowning, Nikki demonstrated by rapidly thrusting her tongue in and out of her mouth.

"That's disgusting," Carole declared. "What did you do?"

"Avoided eye contact — looked above their heads. A guy up front kept rubbing himself during my last trailer. I pointed him out to Marc and out he went. It's good to know they're taking care of me." Nikki's face suddenly grew serious. "They'd *better* take care of me." Forcefully, she kicked her shoes into a corner.

Alarmed at the change of mood, Carole asked, "Will you be able to handle this?"

Nikki reached for her hand. "I feel safe with Marc. He doesn't take any shit." She flexed imaginary muscles. "You saw his size. This may not make sense to you Carole, but I felt the rowdiness of the crowd tonight invading me. It's really a jungle — so different from the polite clapping in L.A. Know what I mean?"

"I think so," Carole said. "It'd be clearer if I could see one show. Will you work on it?"

Nikki drew Carole to her and kissed her. "Hug me. Be near me. This has been the longest day. We made it."

Carole's arms encircled her. Nikki's blouse was drenched with perspiration.

Janice, you were wrong, she thought. Nikki's not the little girl you knew. She's hurdled everything that's come our way.

She squeezed Nikki tighter. "You're so warm. Do you want to change?"

Nikki stepped back. "No. I want you to undress me," she said provocatively. "Do it slowly. Enjoy it."

Whatever uncertainty Carole had about Nikki's intentions was dispelled as soon as she began to disrobe her lover. When their lovemaking ended, an exhausted Carole looked at the window and saw that darkness was surrendering to a gray dawn.

CHAPTER TWENTY-ONE

Journal Entry — Quebec, July 1, 1973

Nikki and I slept till mid-afternoon. I needed the rest after the long flight and especially after our lovemaking — the longest ever. For breakfast we went down to the café for cheese omelettes with raw onions. They sure make strong coffee up here. I'm still wired. Tonight is my second night of lock-up — feels strange.

Back to my journal. I want to record everything. Sometimes I'm my own best company. I keep telling myself there's nowhere for me to go anyway. Besides, it's worth staying in if it keeps Nikki happy.

Today I finally saw Coulterville. The town is the pits. It seems bulldozed flat, like it was thrown together, ready to be taken down again at any moment. Clapboard buildings and nothing over two stories high. No sense of permanence. Reminds me of a trailer park. No one gives a damn, either.

Walking around today I got the feeling that people were working hard not to look at us. Makes me mad. I've never seen Nikki so ignored in my life. She said I should get used to the cold shoulder during the day. The locals pretend they don't know who we are, in spite of their crazy drunken antics at the club at night.

The earth is bright red and barren. The only flowers I saw were tiny daisies planted in cans around the housing projects. That's where the Indians live. Any place where anything can grow there are daisies, so tiny and short they're almost sad — except I wanted to kiss them.

The weather is unbearably hot and humid. High nineties. Even though it was a bitch, Nikki and I walked for miles — two, three hours — till we found the Indians. Talk about squalor. Looks like they got shafted here, too.

I photographed groups of Indian children (their teeth are terrible), playing outside their houses. The kids were eager to have their pictures taken. The front doors were open. We peeked inside and saw grown-ups just sitting around. A radio was playing in the background. Nikki and I tried to give the kids some change, but their mothers came and took them away. Slammed the doors on us. We left when older teenagers started following us around. Scary.

I can't imagine living in a town like this — nothing to do, nowhere to go. The pictures I took seem dead. Have to find a dramatic way of presenting the bleakness of the town, the harshness of Indian life. There must be some sense of community — something I'm not seeing. Have to figure out a way to get beneath what I saw today.

Journal Entry — July 2, 1973

Boy, was Janice ever wrong! Nikki hasn't been moody or weird once. Last night was a repeat of the night before. She's so turned on after work we automatically wind up making love. Sex is different here than at home — more intense — especially for her. Can't figure out why. Maybe the town brutes bring out the animal in her. I never knew she could talk so dirty, or that I would love hearing it so much. Kinky. No complaints.

After breakfast we went to the main shopping district. The guy at the café said the Indians shop at the Hudson Bay Company. Sometimes they sell buckskin dresses to whites. Nikki and I went there. What a disappointment. Hudson Bay is nothing more than a small department store. The Indian women (they're pretty fat) do the shopping while the men wait outside drinking beer. Took some pics of the men, but once they saw me they turned away. They wear cowboy shirts, jeans and work boots. Irony.

Nikki was great. Even though the women speak their own patois, she was able to combine enough French and hand signals to let them know we were interested in buying buckskin dresses. One of them gave us her address. We had no trouble finding it. The street names go from "A" to "M" and "1" to "9."

The woman seemed surprised when we showed up. We had to wait for her to find the dresses. She took two out of a box full of old clothes. Who knows when she made them! The leather was hard and discolored and still reeked of cow. Ugh. The dresses were about size sixteen. There was no way to pretend we liked them.

Nikki held the dress up to her and while she examined it she told the woman we were from California and that I was a photographer who wanted to take pictures of the people in Coulterville. She asked the woman if I could photograph her and her friends. She hesitated, but when Nikki said she would buy the dress, the woman agreed. Nikki paid her thirty dollars. (!!!) We're supposed to return tomorrow.

Journal Entry — July 3, 1973

Third night of lock-up. Last night was a repeat of the last two. I'm sure getting curious about what goes on at that club. Nikki got home mad as a hornet because some guy threw lit matches at her hair while she was on the chair. Marc came to the rescue again, threw the guy out.

After she told me about the evening, she insisted we make love. It was hard for me to get into it, all I could think of was her beautiful hair in flames. But she was adamant about having sex. She was almost rough. She wanted me to slap her. I refused. She grabbed my arm and tried to force me to hit her. The struggle set off something in her. I've never seen her come so fast or so many times. I have a hard time believing it has anything to do with me. It surely can't be Marc. He reminds me of Bluto. All this is messing with my mind. This room is looking smaller all the time.

The photo session with the Indian women was unforgettable. At first, Nikki and I laughed when the woman who sold us the buckskin dresses said her name was Marie. She had three other women with her — all in the one hundred and eighty pound range. They asked for money first. Nikki gave each five dollars. So far, so good.

They wanted to pose outside and seemed upset when I insisted on shooting them indoors. I wanted to capture the mish-mash of furniture. In the living room Marie had a real nice couch next to two small beds — no sheets, only blankets. In the middle of the room was a card table with a radio. Instead of chairs, there were large metal milk containers. I asked them to turn on the radio and out came Paul Anka! Got some nice close-ups of them listening to the radio.

Just as they were starting to relax in front of the camera, one of the husbands came in. He spoke angrily to his wife but pointed his finger at Nikki. I could make out the word "danseuse." Nikki tried to say something but he turned his back on her and glared at his wife until she left the room. He said something more and then the other two women walked out of the house with him. Poor Marie. When she came back, she seemed afraid to look at us. She went into the kitchen and started slamming pots and pans around, probably hinting for us to leave.

Nikki and I were standing alone in the living room. She was livid with anger and demanded that we "get our asses out of here." I told her I didn't care what happened, but I knew I hadn't gotten twenty bucks worth of shooting. Reluctantly, she agreed to stay. I took my time finishing the roll, photographing every detail of the room. I know I'm going to love the results.

Later, I asked Nikki to explain what went wrong at Marie's. She said that as near as she could follow, the man didn't want her in their house because Indians weren't allowed in the club where she danced. I asked Nikki if that was true. She said the manager had told her, "They spit and piss on the floor." I can't believe it.

Journal Entry — July 4, 1973

Today was one of the longest days in my life. It's still hot as hell and Nikki was in a foul mood. Still mad about yesterday's encounter with the Indian. When I told her I agreed with him "in principle," she got mad at me. So then we didn't even have each other to talk to for several hours.

I left her working a crossword puzzle in the café. Shot a couple rolls of the town. Bad scene. A pick-up truck with two guys inside swerved toward me. One of the men stuck his head out and shouted, "Lesbian!" I flipped him the finger and screamed, "Faggot!"

I've never felt so humiliated in my life. How do they know? I went back to the hotel and told Nikki. I couldn't believe her answer. She said, "Lots of strips travel with their girlfriends." That just made me madder. She told me that the manager and everyone else at the club takes it for granted we're lovers. I feel branded. I hate hate hate this shit-hole town.

To make matters worse, she came home after work and wanted sex again. I told her, "Don't get near me." I have an image of the whole town listening with stethoscopes to the walls of our room. Maybe there's little peepholes, like Norman Bates had in Psycho.

Journal Entry — July 5, 1973

Tomorrow is Nikki's last night. Good. These lock-ups drive me crazy. I didn't wait up for her like usual. I was still mad at her when she left for work. How can she be so cool when people just assume we're lesbians? Why am I so uptight? That guy made me feel dirty.

Nikki only made matters worse when she tried to calm me down. She said that when people call her lesbian, she just answers, "Yes." She said I'm having trouble accepting it and that's why I got mad. Maybe she's right. That's what I want to record here — that I'm not comfortable with how we're viewed by the hicks in this town. Everything in L.A. just blends. No one seems to give a fuck. Or maybe I'm braver at home because there's more of us.

She woke me when she got home and apologized for being impatient. She said she had forgotten how shocking that word is when uttered in contempt. She let me talk and get my anger out. I cried. And then she cried and told me she was tired and about to snap. It was good to hear what she was feeling. She was very tender with me — like at home — gentle strokes and kisses. Our lovemaking seemed to come out of ourselves instead of something she dragged in from the goddamn club.

I'm going to sneak out of here tomorrow night and see if I can get into the club. I'll go to the last show and catch a ride home with Nikki and Marc.

CHAPTER TWENTY-TWO

Carole left for the club at midnight. Even though the evening air was warm, heavy, she decided to wear pants and a light jacket. She stuffed her thick curly hair into Nikki's burgundy beret hoping that from a distance she would be taken for a young man and be safe. Before leaving she looked at herself in the mirror and burst out laughing. "Christ! Now I really look like a dyke!"

The half-mile walk seemed much longer. The dim street lamps were irregularly spaced and, at times, she walked in absolute darkness. She hurried, hugging the store fronts that lined the way to the club. A car approached from behind; its headlights caught her; she lowered her head and moved faster. She felt the pounding in her heart, forcing herself to keep a steady pace, as she listened for the car to slow down. When the car finally passed, her stomach and legs were in spasms.

All the capital letters of the neon sign *Le Petite Monde* were burned out. A half-block away she could hear the heavy bass beat of "Borsalino," one of Nikki's songs. The parking lot around the club was crowded — trucks, vans, motorbikes, cars, all of them haphazardly parked.

She pushed open the door, prepared to pay an entrance fee to the person on duty. No one was there. Loud male shouts and thundering music came from behind two heavy green curtains reeking of cigarette and alcohol fumes. She stepped through unnoticed, and stood against the back wall.

The room was packed with men in a drunken frenzy. They shouted, whistled, rubbed their hands across their groins, gyrated toward the stage.

Like a ringmaster, Nikki presided over the bacchanal. She laughed, bumped, teased.

Slowly she slipped off her black-net stocking and offered it to a young man wearing a Montreal Expos baseball cap. Eagerly he reached over the railing; Nikki wrapped the stocking around his neck and tied it into a bow. The young man kissed it. His friends at the table howled like wolves at her and she turned her back on them.

As the last dance started, Carole watched unbelievingly. She saw that Nikki's movements in no way resembled the routine practiced with Janice. Nikki did not draw her knees against her chest, nor did she swivel so that her legs went against the back of the chair. Instead, she thrust her legs forward as if to expose herself. The club pulsed with unrestrained abandon every time she teased.

The audience roared and Nikki threw her head back; she laughed, sensually caressing her breasts and thighs. Her inflamed audience begging for more, she responded by turning her back on them — again.

Unable to watch any longer, Carole rushed out, but found little relief in the hot humid night air. The music ended and she could hear the wild shouting of satiated patrons.

Imagining Nikki bowing lewdly, offering her breasts in gratitude for their lust, Carole pounded her fists on her thighs and muttered, "Goddamn her! Goddamn you Nikki!"

She circled the club to the exit where she guessed Nikki and Marc would soon appear. Her legs were too shaky to carry her back to the motel.

Two men in their mid-thirties leaned against the back door. She kept her head down and stood off to the side. Her head snapped back as her beret suddenly was yanked off.

Twirling the beret on his index finger one of the men taunted, "You're the girlfriend of the dancer, eh?"

"Give that back," Carole demanded. "I don't want any shit from you."

Laughing drunkenly he stuffed the beret in his pocket. His companion grabbed Carole by the hair and jerked her toward him. He thrust his hard groin against her pelvis. "Take fat dick," he said in broken English, grinding his body against her. His fetid breath sickened her.

"Nikki!" Carole screamed. Wildly she struck out and wrenched herself loose from his grip. She ran, stumbled, twisting her ankle over a broken brick. Again she screamed, "Nikki!"

The man jumped on her. She seized the brick and bashed him across his nose and eyes. He reeled, fell away from her, swearing in pain. His companion rushed to help him.

Carole saw a circle of men form around her — the exiting club audience crowding around a new spectacle. They were cheering. Despite the language barrier, she understood that they were urging the men to take her.

I'm not going to let it happen, she swore. She struggled to her feet, still clasping the brick.

The uninjured man leaped at her. The crowd hooted at the one-to-one encounter. Again she screamed, "Nikki!"

The crowd echoed the chant, "Neekee! Neekee!"

The man circled her. She saw his slack-jawed face clearly — his rheumy eyes, his pitted skin. Each time he advanced, she retreated. She saw him study her movements. He feinted toward the twisted ankle, causing her to put her weight on it.

She lost her balance. Before she reached the ground, he had wrested the brick from her. She saw him lift his arm. He struck her once, twice across the face. Blind with pain, covering herself with her arms, she kicked wildly at him.

She heard two gunshots. Behind her attacker, a large silhouette emerged from the exit door. Marc. "Go home! Go home now!" He barked at the crowd. He pointed the gun menacingly at Carole's assailant who seemed unwilling to end his assault.

Partially clad, Nikki lunged from the darkness, wielding a piece of clay pipe. "Pig! Bastard!" she shrieked.

198

She brought the pipe down on his crown. He collapsed, unconscious, landing almost on top of Carole.

"*Merde!*" Marc said. "I hope you didn't kill him."

Fiercely, Nikki struck the man again on the back, legs, face. Marc snatched the pipe from her hands and flung it across the parking lot. Effortlessly, he picked up Nikki with one arm and the bloodied Carole with the other and hauled them into the office.

He said to the manager, "You take care of them. I'm taking the man to the hospital."

Vaguely, Carole heard Nikki order in a rasping voice, "Forget him. Get my girlfriend to the hospital."

Her vision blurred. She saw tears streaming down Nikki's face; Nikki's hands shook as she hovered over Carole.

In a calm voice the manager answered, "I drive you to hospital. Put on clothes," he said to Nikki. "Then we go."

The emergency room doctor sewed stitches under Carole's left eye and left cheek. Nikki refused to leave her side. She demanded that Carole's head and ankle be x-rayed and that she be sedated: "I don't want her in pain."

Carole slept comatose in a hospital room until eight o'clock the next morning when Marc showed up to drive them to the motel. He carried Carole to the room, lay her on the bed, and rested the hospital-issued crutches against the chair.

"Are you still leaving on the four o'clock bus?" he asked.

"We should if I'm to open in Chicoutimi tomorrow night. But I'm afraid to move her. I refuse to leave her alone."

"I think perhaps you should go. She can rest on the bus."

"You've been very nice to me all week, Marc. Thank you." Nikki reached for her purse and gave him twenty dollars.

Marc tipped his hat. "Last night you were a foolish woman. The young girl was foolish, too."

"I hope it won't cause trouble for you. Goodbye Marc."

Nikki rearranged Carole's pillows so that her injuries were untouched by the bedding. She gave Carole two tablets and helped her take them with a glass of water. "Codeine, darling," she whispered, then stretched out at the foot of the bed.

Carole's head and leg throbbed. Unable to open her eye fully she touched her face and felt bandages. Alarmed, she sat up. "What's this?" The sleeping Nikki remained inert.

Carole lay back down, trying to reconstruct the night before. She remembered the crowd around her, and the man's arm with the brick poised above her. She touched her face again. "Oh, Christ," she moaned loudly.

Nikki sat up immediately. "I'm here, darling." She lightly kissed Carole's taped ankle and reached for the medication. "There's more codeine for the pain, if you need it. They took x-rays. You're going to be all right."

"How bad is my face? I can't open my left eye. Tell me the truth!"

Nikki moved closer to Carole and stroked her hand. "You have six stitches under your eye, four on the cheek. The doctor said that once you're healed the marks will eventually fade. He said he took the tiniest stitches possible. I was with you all the time, remember?"

Carole pulled her hand away. "Are you mad at me?"

Taking her hand again, Nikki shook her head. "I can't be mad at you. I'm grateful Marc got there in time."

Carole looked at Nikki. The previous night's makeup was smeared; her eyes looked bruised. "I saw you dance," Carole faltered. "You were . . . obscene."

"You were actually *in* the club?" Nikki looked furious. "Did you come to spy on me?"

"I had to find out why you were so turned on every time you came back."

There was a sharp edge to Nikki's voice. "So? Did you find out?"

"I know I saw something I don't understand. I'm too fucked up right now to figure it out."

Nikki got up and paced the floor. "Let me make it easy for you. I did a hard act all week. I've never done that before in my life, but I had to turn the tables on them if I was going to make it. I wanted them screaming, howling for me. And when they reached for me, I turned my back on them. I controlled them. Yes, I was raunchy. Yes, I was vulgar."

"Why?"

Nikki knelt next to Carole. "It's this place. The men — what they saw in me, what they wanted from me. It's their rawness — a desperation I've never experienced. I had to stay ahead of them. I saw that the first night."

"But why sink to their level?"

Nikki shook her head. "Can't you see that I *didn't?* I saw I was all things to them. I assumed power. Do you know what it's like to have an audience desire you, want you, and while you're on stage, feel their heat *enter* you?" Nikki looked at Carole expectantly.

Carole shrugged in frustration.

Nikki's voice rose. She spoke rapidly. "Don't you see? They would've taken me if I'd let them. All I had was myself and Marc, but *I* had to do something to keep them at bay. The sweet, mincy dance I did at home would never have held them here. They're away from home, too. No wives. No girlfriends. Just booze and work and nowhere to let it out."

"I saw them. They were animals." Impulsively Carole lifted her head, forgetting her wounds. She gasped and lay back.

"Yes, they were animals — but under my control." Nikki steadied her breathing and moved onto the bed. "I've been under a strange kind of madness all week."

She continued softly, "It's been torture. I've wanted to tell you about it but there was no way to explain it. I'm glad you saw it. Every night I trembled wondering if I would be able to win the game one more time."

A loud rap on the door caused them to jump.

"Who is it?" Nikki called.

"Police."

"Aha! The missing ingredient," Carole said sarcastically.

"Please don't say anything," Nikki whispered. She opened the door.

Two Coulterville officers stood in the doorway. "Are you Nicole Donato?" asked the taller of the two.

"How can I help you?"

"Nicole *Donato?*" gasped Carole. She forced herself to sit upright.

"This is Officer Hontax. He does not speak English. My name is Michaud. May we come in?"

"Of course," Nikki said coolly. "This is Carole Wolston, my traveling companion."

Carole nodded.

Michaud asked, "Nikki, may I see your work papers, please?"

She walked to the closet and gave him an envelope. "Everything is in order, I assure you."

Michaud carefully studied the papers. "Yes, but I must take these from you until some matters are cleared up. Your permit to work is, for the time being, revoked. I must ask you to come with us to the station."

"I would like an explanation," Nikki said.

Michaud stood stiffly; his voice assumed a deep formal tone. "A complaint of assault and battery has been made against you by a Mr. Alain Germaine. He is in the hospital in serious condition."

"Look what he did to me!" Carole shouted. She pointed to her bandaged face and ankle.

Ignoring Carole and reading from a yellow form, Michaud stated, "Mr. Germaine has a cracked skull, spine injuries and a broken left shin bone."

Gesturing angrily at Carole, Nikki demanded, "Did Mr. Germaine tell you that he and his friend were beating her with a brick? Her face is cut, her ankle's twisted. Look at the bruises on her arms."

"She saved my life," Carole protested. "If it weren't for her, they'd have killed me."

"Mr. Germaine has witnesses. If you wish, you may come to the station to file a counter-complaint."

"Believe me, I will," Carole declared.

Michaud turned to Nikki. "I'm sorry Mrs. Donato, you must come with us now."

"May I have a few moments to wash my face and change my clothes? It's been a long night. You can wait right outside the room. I'm not going anywhere. I promise."

The officers stepped outside. Quickly, Nikki took out a sheet of paper and wrote down three phone numbers. "Honey, I know you feel shitty, but this has got to be done *right now!* This first number is Bert's private number. This other one is the office number. When you get hold of him tell him *exactly* what happened. Give him the names of the two arresting officers and that creep, Alain Germaine. He's at Mercy Hospital. I'm writing everything down for you."

Carole asked weakly, "Nikki, are you really married to Bert?"

"Just on paper, honey. I'll explain later. There's no time. Bert has people in Montreal. We've got to get out of this town."

Carole sighed. "What else?"

"If, for some reason, you can't get hold of Bert, call Janice and tell her exactly what happened. She'll find him. Make sure you give her all the names, too."

Hurriedly Nikki washed, changed her clothes, and touched up her face. Carole watched her, noting that her face showed no sign of nervousness, no evidence that she had not eaten or slept for twenty-four hours.

As Nikki opened the door, the reality of being left alone and the course of action that lay before her filled Carole with panic. "Nikki!" she called.

Nikki gazed at her from the doorway. Carole was quieted by the look of love that flowed from Nikki's blue eyes.

"Thank you for waiting, gentlemen," Nikki said. The door closed softly.

CHAPTER TWENTY-THREE

Carole hobbled on crutches to the café where she and Nikki had breakfasted all week. The owner offered to lead her to a booth, but Carole shook her head. She spoke slowly. "I need to use the telephone — emergency, long distance." She held out a twenty dollar bill. "I need lots of change."

He surveyed her swollen ankle and bandaged face. "All this was from last night?"

"You heard?"

"Coulterville is very small," he said, almost apologetically. "You use my phone to make your calls. No change possible. Ask operator. You pay me. My phone is in the kitchen." The café owner placed a chair next to a wall phone.

Working through the long distance operator, Carole located Donato at his private number. He answered after the second ring. "Bert, this is Carole, Nikki's girlfriend."

"What's the problem?"

Carole reported the story in exacting detail as Nikki had requested. She spelled out the names of the arresting officers and Alain Germaine, the attacker who had pressed charges against Nikki.

"Bert." Her voice trembled. "My face is cut up. I'm bruised. My ankle is taped. When I get off the phone, I'm going down to the police station and swear out a complaint. The bastard . . ." She swallowed to keep her voice from breaking.

"No, Carole," Bert said. "This is what you do. Go back right now to the motel and wait for Nikki. She'll be there in two or three hours. Pack. Get ready to move as soon as she gets there."

"Why should I let him get away with this?" Carole argued. "I want to press charges. Bert, you should *see* me."

He spoke slowly, firmly. "Do as I say. It's for your protection, for Nikki's protection. Believe me, I know what I have to do. Now you do what you have to do."

Carole had barely finished packing when a knock sounded at the door. "Honey, let me in."

Carole hopped on her good foot to open the door. Marc stood next to Nikki, who held out her arms. Carole fell into them. "You're all right, aren't you?" Tears of relief filled Carole's eyes. "You're here, just like Bert said."

"They let me go." Nikki hugged Carole. "Here, lean on me." She guided her to the bed, then looked around the room. "You've done so much hard work. It must have been difficult. Come on in, Marc. Carole has the suitcases ready."

Marc carried out the luggage. He closed the door, leaving Nikki and Carole alone.

"Did Bert fix things?" Carole asked, impatient to know everything. "Tell me what happened."

"Charges were dropped. Marc is driving us to Chicoutimi. We'll get there faster and you'll be more comfortable than on the bus." Carefully, Nikki stroked Carole's face and hair. She kissed her bruised face and wiped away the tears.

Carole sighed, rested her head on Nikki's chest. "Those sons-of-bitches attacked me and now they're going to get away with it." She released all emotion. Her loud sobs filled the room.

Nikki held her tightly, rocked her. "Yes, darling, cry. It's so unfair . . " She also burst into tears. She buried her head into Carole's hair, repeatedly kissing her.

Carole allowed herself to be consoled and gained strength from being able to comfort Nikki. "I feel better now. How about you?" She took Nikki's hand. "You still haven't had any sleep."

"I'll sleep during the drive. Let's get moving, darling."

"Is everything all right? You're not keeping anything from me, are you?"

Nikki kissed Carole. "Bert's wiring money to the club owner. Everybody's getting paid off."

"Even that creep, Germaine?"

"Yes."

"Shit! He beat me up and he's getting money to boot? Does that mean I'm expendable?"

Nikki put her hands on Carole's shoulders. "No, it means we have to leave town while we can. And from now on we'll have to toe the line."

Embarrassed, Carole nodded. "You mean, *I* have to toe the line."

"It's my fault too," Nikki admitted. "I should have let you in on what was happening with me. I felt cornered — my back to the wall. It's over — gone — passed." She rose and brought Carole's crutches. "I'll carry the rest. We need to leave *now!*"

"But," Carole protested. "When are you going to tell me about you and Bert?"

"Later. I promise."

Marc's '68 blue Oldsmobile gleamed brightly. The trunk, bulging with Nikki's luggage, was tied down. Carole lay on the back seat. Nikki made a makeshift pillow out of their coats and elevated Carole's ankle. "You'll be more comfortable this way. I'll ride in the front with Marc."

Carole asked, "When will we get there?"

He started the motor. "Three hours."

"Good," Nikki said. "I'll have time to rest before I open tonight."

Pain pierced Carole's chest at the memory of Nikki stripping. It brought back the anguish of the night before. Yesterday, had that been only yesterday? She touched her face. How will I look once the bandages are removed? Hate rushed through her as the features of her assailant flashed before her.

* * * * *

The Showboat, Nikki's next stop, was attached to a restaurant and their hotel. Situated in the paved downtown district of Chicoutimi, the club was adjacent to a residential district dotted with red brick homes. Large maple trees shaded the streets.

Nikki and Carole's room was well-equipped: a telephone with a hotel directory, television, bathroom with tub and shower and plenty of towels, writing desk with stationery, pens and a Gideon Bible in the drawer. The pale rose bedspread looked recently laundered.

Nikki helped Carole to a chair. She smiled, her arms outstretched as she presented the room. "What do you think? I told you the worst was behind us."

Carole agreed, sarcastically. "Yes, this *cell* will be much more comfortable than the last one."

Playfully, Nikki tousled Carole's hair. "Hey, don't talk that way. This is a regular club. There's no reason why you can't come watch the show."

Carole pointed to her bandages and smirked. "Sure, I look so great." She threw off her clothes and hopped into bed.

Nikki unpacked a T-shirt and tossed it to her. "I'm dead tired. And I've still got tonight's show to worry about. I've got to sleep." She picked up the phone and asked to be called at nine p.m. "First thing tomorrow, Carole," Nikki yawned, "we'll have our talk." She undressed and slid under the covers.

"I'll hold you to it. My head's screwed up — inside and out."

Nikki sat up. "You don't doubt my love, do you?"

"No, nor is my love for you in question. I'm confused because I thought I knew you — now I'm not so sure."

209

"You *do* know me. And if my past is more important to you than the person I am now, then the past I shall give you." Nikki lay back down, stretched lazily. "Please, no more until tomorrow."

Carole roused gradually. She lifted her hand to her bandages. "It's throbbing again. Where's the codeine?"

"Next to you on the nightstand," Nikki replied. "Why not wait till you have something in your stomach? I've already ordered room service."

The morning sun poured in as Nikki pulled back the drapes. She looked out from their third story window and sighed audibly. "Real people. Men and women. Real stores. Real streets."

An hour later, Nikki set the room service tray out in the hall. She settled comfortably in a chair and propped her feet on the bed. "Okay. About my past. The part you're interested in begins with Bert. He started out as a club owner in the midwest. When Janice and I met him, he was already well-established with clubs and everything that went with them — mainly prostitution and gambling."

Carole noted how matter-of-factly Nikki had spoken those two words. "What about drugs?"

"None. At least not that I ever saw. Drugs meant instant deportation — Bert wasn't a citizen then." Nikki curled her legs under her. "At that time, Racehorse Dick was one of the managers at Bert's club in Chicago where I was working. He kept saying, 'The big gun is coming. I want you girls out hustling drinks. No lagging around in the dressing room after the show.'

"Rumors were the big gun was Vinnie, a supposed nephew of Lucky Luciano, from East Kansas City. He took a liking to me. He was a good-looking guy dressed in a black suit and white silk shirt and tie — stocky build, about forty-two — looked more Greek than Italian. He told me he'd had six wives — all of them strippers and he'd named his clubs after each one of them. Vinnie said he was leaving for Brazil that night. He wanted me to come with him and be his seventh wife. He promised he'd name his next club after me. I was terrified."

"Why? You didn't really believe him, did you?"

Nikki shook her head. "Carole, this is the Mob we're talking about. The guy was in the club peeling off hundred dollar bills and throwing them over the bar like they were dirty napkins. Two bodyguards stood behind him. Yes, I believed him."

Amazed, Carole looked at Nikki for a long time. "You're so secretive. If something like that happened to me, I'd tell you the first two hours we met. Why did you keep this from me?"

"They aren't memories I like to keep alive. They're painful. That was the worst time in my life. The only friend I had at work was Millie, a B-girl in her mid-fifties. Her job was to sit there and drink with the customers. I remember she arrived every night wearing a pill-box hat and skimpy mink stole." Nikki laughed. "I haven't thought of her in years."

Carole laughed with her. "Real mink?"

"Yes, probably the first one ever sewn together. Getting back to Vinnie, I was naive, scared, and in incredible danger. He wouldn't take my no's seriously. He was sure he'd convince me by the time he got me to the airport. He ordered his bodyguard to carry me to the car. So this guy just picked me up and tossed me over his shoulder. I was screaming, trying to climb down."

Nikki clenched her fists and hit her legs as if re-living the experience. "Customers, strippers, everybody just stood there with their mouths open. Suddenly, Millie jumped the bodyguard, hit him with her purse, began yelling that I was just a baby and didn't want to go. Then the others began yelling, too. Finally Vinnie ordered his man to let me go."

Carole leaned back on the bed pillows. She looked at Nikki and acutely felt their differentness. Nikki knew how to deal with the outsiders of society, while she herself observed them — behind the safety of her camera. In reality she'd always been part of the mainstream. She saw that she'd been deluding herself when she had walked through the ghettos of L.A. photographing street people. She had not stepped into their world at all. She had paid a safe visit.

She could not dwell on this now. She pressed Nikki, "Where does your marriage to Bert fit into all this?"

"Hold on. It's coming. Good old Vinnie didn't give up. He threatened to send his people for me and finally Racehorse Dick told Bert what was happening."

"How well did you know Bert then?"

"Casually, from working in the club. Bert came to see me and Janice at the hotel and laid his cards on the table. He said he needed an American wife and an alibi for a certain date and time. He said the only way to solve my problem with Vinnie was if I were married to a business associate. They respected each other's wives."

"Did he know you were gay?"

"We told him. He didn't care. The deal was, he'd keep Vinnie and others away from me. All I had to do was marry him and not ask questions. I went along."

Carole narrowed her eyes. "Had he killed somebody?"

"Of course not."

Carole couldn't contain herself. She shouted, "You don't know that. He wouldn't have told you. Maybe you were an accomplice to a murder. How could you know if you didn't ask questions?"

As if to steady herself, Nikki took a deep breath and lowered her voice. "He told me people were trying to frame him. I believed him. No charges were ever brought against him. So I never had to testify. Bert was protecting himself—just in case. I was helping him. He was helping me. Vinnie left me alone. After that, Bert made sure I got booked into top clubs."

Carole shook her head, ran her fingers through her unruly curls. "I don't understand why you're still married. More than enough time has passed for you to divorce him."

"I agree," Nikki said. "But it's been more convenient for us to stay married. Men leave me alone. And he can have the women he wants and not be pressed for a commitment. He's a loyal friend, Carole. He's never forgotten the favor. He's made sure I always have a job."

She held Carole's eyes with her gaze. "He's very proud of my going to the university. That's why he helps with the tuition. Bert's been very kind to me."

Carole wrinkled her nose in disgust. "I think it's weird. You work for this shady character and you never told me. What's more, you're still his wife!"

Nikki said hotly, "Bert is not shady, Carole. He's worked damn hard and he's come a long way. Not all of us have things handed to us. It's very easy for you to judge."

Carole bristled. "Are you saying I've had things handed to me?"

"I'm saying you don't know what it's like to put yourself on the line to save your hide. I wanted to be an actress. I wanted a life of glamour. I thought stripping

213

would get me what I wanted. Even *that's* turned out to be a bitch. Back when I started, the clubs were controlled by strong men who used us as mannequins. Nothing's been easy."

Nikki paced the floor for a few moments, then stopped abruptly. Her eyes focused on the panoramic picture of the Canadian Rockies above the bed. "People who chase success or glamour make compromises. Judge me if you want to, Carole, but I warn you, I won't hang my head in shame to you or anybody. I did what I had to, to stay alive."

"Was stripping your only alternative?" Carole challenged her.

"You still don't get it," Nikki retorted angrily. "Stripping was what I *wanted* to do. I didn't *want* to be a bank teller. I didn't *want* to go to secretarial school. I didn't *want* to be a PBX trainee. I *wanted* makeup and applause, lights and music. I'll leave stripping without ever reaching my real dream. I'm going to miss it terribly!" Nikki buried her face in her hands.

Carole struggled out of bed toward Nikki. "Don't," she pleaded. "Don't cry. I'm not judging you. Truly, I'm not."

Nikki pulled away. "You can't help yourself. Your road was carefully paved for you. Bert and I came up a lonely back road with nothing but our wits to help us. He's made it. His success is as worthy as anyone's. I'm trying to make it, too."

Nikki managed a smile. "In a way Bert and I *are* married to each other — with all the benefits and none of the drawbacks."

CHAPTER TWENTY-FOUR

Four nights after Nikki opened at the Showboat in Chicoutimi, Carole was still in bed, refusing to watch her dance, or to make herself known to the club manager and other personnel.

Nikki arranged for meals from room service, ordering special treats for her. "This is a real hamburger. Try it." Touched by Nikki's concern, Carole nibbled half-heartedly. She was moved by Nikki's persistence to bring her out of her retreat. But she remained non-communicative. She refused to tour the town or have visitors come to the room. All she wanted was to have Nikki hold her.

She had no qualms about anyone seeing her cuts and bruises, nor was she indulging in self-pity. She remained cloistered trying to understand Nikki's tearful outburst over her upcoming retirement from the stripping circuit.

How could it matter that much? She recalled how derisive she had been when Nikki told her, with honest pride, that she had been a stripper for twelve years. Carole cringed, remembering her own shallowness, remembering how she thought it incredible, even ridiculous, that such a beautiful woman could willingly have been a stripper for so long.

She wondered: What would I have done in a similar situation? Nikki's right, my road was paved for me. The one path I can honestly say I've traveled on my own was to reach Nikki's love, and I would have pursued that no matter what the consequences. Maybe at first I was lured by her exotic world, but now it doesn't matter anymore. I still wish she wasn't tied to Bert — it binds me too. I don't like it.

Her reservations about Nikki's past and Nikki's relationship with Bert lessened as she recalled how easily she herself had fallen into Nikki's realm, how easily she had been seduced by the gloss of painted women who sat backstage, played Scrabble, pieced together jigsaw puzzles, and talked ceaselessly of their finances, their patch-work love lives, their dreams of meeting Mr. Right, of being discovered. Yes, they spoke. They opened their hearts to each other. They confided only in each other, with the candor reserved for strangers or father-confessors.

216

At first she had been awed by their conversations. She could envision a young Nikki listening in similar awe to a worldly Janice spinning tales about how wonderful their lives were going to be. She herself had fallen under Janice's spell. But Nikki had held onto her dream — for *twelve years,* Carole realized.

She recalled how quickly she had become bored with the dancers' monotones, with their repetitive patter about their constant six-week courses, their would-be hopes, and their sure-bets. She felt no such boredom with Nikki. Nikki was different.

She conjured Nikki's image before her — the porcelain skin framed by soft red hair, the steady gaze of the shade-changing blue eyes. She saw no blemish anywhere on her lover's face — no evidence of hardship, danger, of social disapproval because she was a lesbian or a stripper.

Like Dorian Gray, did Nikki have a portrait of herself somewhere? Was there somewhere she could see her soul?

Christ, I'm getting melodramatic. She pursued the idea. Do I believe in a soul? There must be a core to a person though I have no name for it. I know there's something beyond the mind — something like a vial that holds within it all that a person really is.

She looked at the clock. Almost two a.m. Nikki was doing her last show and would be upstairs in half an hour. Carole washed her face and combed her hair.

She feared broaching the subject of Nikki's marriage to Bert. This marriage business had changed everything. The legal aspects of the arrangement bothered her less than Nikki's obvious loyalty and admiration for Bert.

She had been exploding with curiosity to know more about Nikki's early days in stripping and with Bert; she dared not ask, nor had Nikki volunteered anything.

217

Carole suspected that Nikki regretted revealing even the details that she had.

But I love you all the more for having lived through that.

She closed her eyes as she heard the key in the door. She heard the swishing of costumes as Nikki threw them over the chair. There was light in the bathroom; Nikki was removing her makeup before coming to bed.

The warm nakedness pressed against Carole took her off-guard; for the last few nights there had been little sexual contact. The feeling of Nikki against her made her realize how much she hungered for the physical part of their relationship. Not wanting to react too quickly, she lay still, waiting for another cue.

She felt her T-shirt edge up slowly and then Nikki's warm moist mouth caressing the exposed part of her back. Carole lay in silence, and when she could hold back no longer, she sat up and pulled off her top, offering her breasts. Stirred by the familiar circling of her nipples, Carole reached out and urged Nikki's legs apart. Nikki offered no resistance — and Carole discovered her lover flooding with ardor.

She tried to summon body strength to answer Nikki's beckoning, but movement was still painful.

"Carole," said Nikki hoarsely, "Let me give you pleasure. I need to." She guided her to the pillows.

"Nikki, I've needed you ..." Her body pulsing, she lay back and savored Nikki's gentleness as it pushed aside the pain, leaving only ecstasy and fulfillment.

The club's night sounds had ended and only an occasional hotel door slam broke the silence. In the dark room she rested comfortably in Nikki's arms. "I've missed you. I've been going through these bad head trips."

Nikki gave her a light squeeze. "I could tell."

"You've been so patient," Carole said. "Tell me what's on your mind."

"You. Me. Us. The trip and what it's doing to us. We're not talking much — but we're closer. The inner part of ourselves is closer. I hurt every time I look at your wounds. We've been through a lot."

"Yes — the beating, having to race out of town like *we* were the ones who did something wrong. I've been pushed about as far as I can go." She leaned close to Nikki. "I have to try and forget about it." She faltered. "Just like I have to accept what you told me about yourself. I need to learn the meaning of trust in love."

"Are you saying you don't trust our love?"

She fumbled for the right words. "I mean, I've decided to trust that whatever you've done is all right."

"You've got some hang-ups to work through." Nikki kissed her. "I'm patient. You're worth waiting for."

She returned the kiss. "I've been afraid to ask. How's this club — compared to the last one?"

"I'm dancing the way you saw me rehearse with Janice, if that'll make you feel better," she said dryly. "Sorry," she added quickly. She kissed Carole's hand. "There's lots of women around here — the men don't have to act like cannibals." She was silent for a few moments. "You've distanced yourself from me all week. You asked questions. I gave answers you didn't like." Nikki sighed. "You say you're struggling to accept me and everything I've done, but I wonder if deep down you haven't lost all your respect for me."

Nikki's straightforwardness jarred Carole. She was afraid of talking about what had plagued her these past days. "I don't know if respect is the word. I don't know what it is." Carole searched within. Yes, she finally admitted, Nikki's suspicion about respect was exactly what she'd been asking herself.

"It's strange to love you so much and realize you've done things I'd never be capable of. Nikki, it frightens me to think of our future."

Her voice almost pleading, Nikki asked, "What are you afraid of? My future is with you — only with you."

Filled with love and yearning for her, Carole forced herself to ask, "What about Bert? Will he be part of our future, too?"

Nikki looked surprised. "He's got nothing to do with us. His business dealings are with me. What bothers you?"

Carole realized that she had been disturbed by Nikki's apparent need to be accountable to this man. A strange kind of jealousy, she thought. I wish I didn't know so much about Nikki and Bert.

"I like Bert," she said cautiously. "I don't like the obligations you have to him. It seems like he'll be an extra person in our lives. You seem so dependent on him."

Nikki was visibly irked. "I work for him. I get a salary. We care a great deal for each other, but our business arrangement is not written in concrete. Are you asking me to sever my relationship with Bert?"

As she heard Nikki's question, she knew Nikki had hit the crux of her uneasiness. She admitted that she wanted Nikki all to herself. She drew herself up and spoke with conviction. "Not the friendship. The business arrangement."

Nikki picked up a brush and ran it through her hair several times. "I've thought about life without Bert. I wonder how practical it would be. He most certainly doesn't need me. If I break with him, the lifestyle I'd offer you wouldn't be easy." She rested her head on Carole's shoulder. "I haven't paid my own rent in a long time."

"I'm not asking you to support me." Excited, Carole volunteered, "I'll give up my apartment — my darkroom. I'll print at school. Things will be tight for us, but only till we finish school." She snuggled closer. "I love you. I'll always love you. My biggest fear is whether I'll be able to handle problems that come our way. I fell apart when I saw you dancing at the last club. I don't want to let you down that way again. I'm haunted by the way I acted."

Nikki set Carole back on the pillows. "Who can promise you a problem-free future? I can't."

"You make me sound like a coward."

Nikki picked up the alarm clock. "It's four-thirty. We can't solve everything tonight." She kissed Carole's forehead. "Let's go to sleep."

"Room service." The rap on the door was loud, the young woman's voice impatient.

Startled, Carole lifted her head to look at the clock. "My God, I forgot I ordered breakfast," she said to Nikki.

The other side of the bed was empty.

There was a louder rap.

"Yes. I'm coming!" Carole shouted. She threw on a robe, fumbled through her purse for some change and ushered in the teen-aged maid carrying the breakfast tray.

Disturbed by Nikki's absence, she ignored the eggs and toast. She sipped coffee and scanned the room for a note. Nothing. She sat immobile for two hours while uneasiness turned to foreboding and the foreboding turned to dread.

When she heard the key in the door, she allowed herself to cry. "Where the hell have you been?" she sobbed.

Nikki rushed to her, embraced her, kissed away the tears. "I'm sorry. You were sleeping so soundly I thought I'd be back before you woke up."

Carole let Nikki rock her awhile. "You could've left a note. It's been awful sitting here."

Nikki pulled up a chair. "Darling, listen carefully —"

Carole interrupted. "It's something bad, isn't it?"

"No, I think it's something good," Nikki said tenderly. "I've given this a lot of thought . . ."

Carole blurted, "What's *this?* Tell me quick."

"The bottom line is, I think you should go back home — to Portland — until I finish the tour."

"Why are you sending me away?"

Nikki held Carole's hands tightly. "I'm not sending you away. But I think we should separate for now. Last night I realized you need time to think things through. You need to resolve your doubts in a safe place. You can't do it in a hotel room. I want you to do it where you feel safe, secure."

"How is that going to get rid of my fears?" cried Carole.

"In Oregon you'll be surrounded by people you know, people you love. You're hurt — you need to heal — you need someone to care for you. I can't do that and work too." Nikki picked up a napkin from the table and wiped Carole's tears. "If you stay here I can't guarantee some other dreadful thing isn't going to happen."

Carole asked angrily, "What dreadful thing? Didn't you say that from now on the clubs would get better?"

"They will. But Carole, it's only the facilities that will improve. You've been locked in your room all week and haven't seen what's going on — the hooking, the drugs."

"Here?" Carole challenged in disbelief.

"Yes! Here! It's heartbreaking. The waitresses come in at two in the afternoon dressed in skimpy little outfits." Nikki paced the floor. "Once an hour they have to use their own coins for the jukebox and do a topless go-go for three songs. If someone wants to get laid, a waitress takes him upstairs, turns a trick, goes back down and continues serving."

"That is terrible. But why should I be sent home because these other women are turning tricks? We have prostitutes in Oregon — and drugs, too."

"Yes, but not as blatant. Every night the girls buy from a seedy ninety-pound guy who comes backstage hawking them. It's disgusting. When people are drugged, they're dangerous. Maybe you feel you can take care of yourself but I don't want to take any chances. Go home. Get well. Work on your pictures."

"Let's get a few things straight." Carole spoke forcefully. "One, I don't want to work on pictures. Two, I get stronger every day. Three, I don't need you to take care of me. I'm not afraid to see what these girls do with their lives. Yes, I admitted I was frightened about us, but I don't want to leave you. What about our love? Aren't you worried?"

"Speaking for myself, I trust my love to last a summer. I had planned a lifetime. How about you?"

Carole saw in Nikki a look of determination she had never seen: the set mouth, the emotionless eyes. "There's nothing I can say that will make you change your mind, is there?"

Nikki shook her head slowly. She sighed. "You're in no shape, physically or emotionally, to think about our future. I've made the arrangements, I bought your ticket to Portland this morning. I want you to go home and decide from there if you want to accept me and make your life with me — without trying to change me. I want you to look at things the way they are."

Carole cradled herself against Nikki's breast. "I'm afraid to go. I'm afraid if I do, something in me will die."

Nikki kissed her. "Then perhaps it was meant to — although I don't think it will. There's something special in you, Carole, something that reminds me of my younger self, a part I lost and found again through you. Trust that I'm making the right decision for us."

CHAPTER TWENTY-FIVE

"Good evening ladies and gentlemen. Welcome aboard Air Canada Flight seven forty-five to Chicago. This is Captain Garey. We'll be cruising at an altitude of thirty thousand feet. Our estimated time of arrival is four-thirty p.m. The weather at O'Hare is in the mid-eighties . . ."

The plane climbed; Carole watched the reality that had once been larger than herself recede, reduce, shrink into impersonal geometric networks: cars and freeways became dots and lines; buildings and homes became rectangles and squares.

She removed her sunglasses, then rested her forehead against the window. The plane's reverberation irritated her still-injured cheekbone. She leaned back to reflect over her last day and a half with Nikki.

Each woman had been solicitous of the other, but Carole had been adamant about making the bus trip from Chicoutimi to Montreal by herself. "If you take me, I'll feel like a child. If I go alone, I'll feel like I'm going on my own steam. Besides, I'm afraid of making a scene at the airport."

Their last night together they had slept in each other's arms, Nikki's grip around Carole's waist strong, as if she were trying to impress herself onto her. She felt Nikki's silent weeping. The one time she tried to speak, Nikki tenderly placed her hand over Carole's mouth.

From the vantage point of distance, she could see that silence was Nikki's way of easing into their parting — no words that could be misconstrued, no last minute resentments levied — just the two of them, pressing closely, feeling the softness, the warmth of each other's body, and from that, drawing the succor to last until they would meet again. When Carole boarded the bus for Montreal, Nikki's magic of the night before stayed with her.

She looked at her watch. Including the two hour layover in Chicago, it would take eleven hours to reach home.

Thank God I'll be arriving at midnight — too late for a family talk. Why do I feel as if they'll take one look at me and know all I've been doing this past year? She looked down at her still-swollen leg and laughed at herself. Life for me will have to be slow for a while. I'm going to hate being dependent.

She dozed until she heard the Fasten Seat Belts request. Inside O'Hare, she hobbled to the United Airlines terminal where, because of her taped ankle, she was allowed to board early.

Airborne, she took out her journal. She shuddered as she read some of her last entries — that week of being locked up in Coulterville. Nikki's strange behavior. Their bizarre sexual interactions. She wrote:

Journal Entry — July 15, 1973

Dear Nikki,

I don't want to talk to myself, so I'm talking to you. It seems strange to be alone after months of being inseparable from you. I'm glad we're not in the same city, because I couldn't keep myself from running to you. There's a numbness somewhere in me. I don't feel like myself without you.

I need your eyes to see me.

Right now you're at work. What are you thinking about? Have you started to miss me yet? I hope you're right about the separation — that it will be good for me. You were worried not only about my body — I suspect — but about my mind as well. At least I hope you were worried, and not tired of me. Was I a drag? Embarrassing. I see me hiding in my room, pouting about your past — as if it were any of my business.

I was a judgmental ass.

I'll be home in a few hours. I'm sad because right now I don't feel I can tell my family of my love for you. I'm afraid to share you — the most important part of my new life —

with my family, the most important part of my past. I'm a
coward and a hypocrite.

There's no way of predicting how they might react.
Liberal as they are, they're still Jewish. I've been away for
two years. They must have gone through changes, too. My
nightmare is that Amy will be hurt. Hard-shelled,
soft-centered Dad will be silent and heartbroken — his
pain the most difficult for me to handle. At the same time,
he's the one I most want to tell about you. I know he'd love
you. He loves beautiful women. It's hard to imagine what
Mom might do. Will her fierce liberal politics extend to me?
Or are they limited to Jane Fonda and the Vietnam war?

I'm going to order a Bloody Mary and while I sip it,
I'm going to lie back and think of you. The future will
decide if I ever show this to you.

The plane touched down and taxied to the terminal.
Carole saw a green landscape obscured by drizzle. She
waited until all passengers had deplaned before she rose.
The stewardess helped her with her carry-on luggage.

"Carole!" Amy bounded up to her, arms outstretched.
"You're hurt. What happened?"

Carole hugged her. "A car accident. It's not as bad as
it looks. I'll be okay."

Amy laughed. "That's funny. I was rear-ended last
week. Wait till the folks see you. Maybe now they'll get off
my back." She took Carole's photo gear from her. "We
won't have to walk in the rain — Mon and Dad are
waiting in the car outside of baggage. He got her a new
Buick — a blue Riviera. Yecch!" She asked, "How much
stuff do you have?"

"A lot. I'll point it out."

Carole looked at her sister closely. Instinctively she knew that she had started her sex life. Amy was now seventeen, and her carriage was more self-assured; she was more attractive. Her long straight auburn hair reached the middle of her back. Eyeliner accentuated her large dark almond-shaped eyes.

They loaded the luggage on a cart and headed into the now heavy rain. Her father's copper-colored beard immediately caught her surprised eye. A contrast to his thick black hair, the beard emphasized an already prominent jawline. With this new look his normal aggressive stride seemed even stronger. Briskly he loaded the trunk. In response to Carole's eager "Hi Daddy," he motioned his daughters to hurry into the car. She had forgotten about Daddy's business-first, fun-later manner.

In the car Carole immediately assured her parents that her injuries were not permanent. Half-listening to the family news, she studied her mother. She too had a new look. Was the hair lighter? She looked younger — still prettier than Amy and herself. She watched her mother take a tissue and affectionately wipe rain off her husband's forehead. She noted an emerald and diamond ring she'd never seen before.

Closer to home, she thought she felt a conspiratorial silence between her parents. She was sure of it when her mother unhooked her seatbelt to turn around and address her directly.

"Carole dear, as you know, we didn't expect you so suddenly, but we're happy to see you. I forgot to tell you that Amy's moved into your old room. And Dad turned hers into an office for himself —"

Carole cut in, "The couch is good enough. Don't worry about me. It's just good to be home."

"How long are you staying, honey?" asked her father.

229

"What's the difference, Dad?" snapped Amy. "She can bunk with me. My friends crash there all the time."

"Quiet, Amy," he said patiently. "Carole, I fixed up the den for you. We hardly ever use it anymore. You'll be comfortable there."

"Wherever you put me is fine. So Dad, what's with the beard?"

Amy clapped and laughed. "Like it? It was my idea. I think it makes him look so sexy."

Her mother chuckled. "Pity there's so much grey in it." She gave the beard a playful tug.

They laughed, savoring what appeared to be an inside joke. Carole felt uncomfortable, left out. She busied herself with finding familiar landmarks on the way to their suburban home. She resented the rainy night; it kept her from seeing the soft green landscape that for years had meant home. Then the car was pulling into the familiar winding driveway bordered by tall cypress.

Her mother helped Carole into the house. The power of the arm around her waist took Carole off guard. Her mother was at least five inches shorter than Carole — her strength seemed incongruous with her height and slight frame.

Lights were on throughout the house. Looking at the gleaming many-paneled glass breakfront containing her mother's Waterford crystal, and the gilt wood of the flower-patterned furniture, Carole smiled to herself. She had never really seen the ostentation of her family. She knew that Nikki would love her house.

She was touched by her father's efforts to convert the spacious family room into something cozy on one day's notice. The coffee table had been turned into a nightstand, complete with lamp and local paper, the TV moved to the foot of the bed. The foldaway couch was against the wall so that she could use the cushions as a backrest. The telephone, however, was far away, on the bar. She controlled her impulse to run to it. She would call Nikki in the morning.

She scanned the room. Her mother's tennis trophies had multiplied as had her father's plaques for community involvement. Her parents' penchant for perfection was maddening. The low cholesterol couple that went to the dentist twice a year and always wore seatbelts. Antiseptic.

Next to her parents' achievements were Amy's numerous riding ribbons and two of Carole's prize-winning photos. The huge family photo taken at her bat mitzvah still held the place of honor on the wall, the beaming faces of her mom and dad contrasting sharply with Amy and Carole's self-conscious smiles; Amy was gap-toothed and Carole wore braces. An embarrassing time, she recalled.

Feeling guilty at her unwillingness to acknowledge her family's warmth, their successes, the smooth life they had carved out for themselves, Carole promised to be more accepting of them.

Am I so different than they? I too, want success. When life got rough for me, I fell apart. Nikki knew what she was doing when she sent me home. Am I weak? Do I *need* my family like she says I do? Yes I was happy to see them — more than I thought I would be. They're nice, pretty people. I'm fortunate to have them. Why do I feel encumbered by them? My true fear is that my life with Nikki will seem sordid from their point of view.

I need Nikki. The world seems shitty without her.

Her arms ached with the desire to wrap themselves around Nikki.

I want her here with me, with everyone knowing what she means to my life.

I want to tell them.

She looked again at her family's symbols of accomplishment. *They're strong people. They can handle it.*

Alone with the heaviness of decision, Carole tossed, turned, tried to distract herself by reading the paper. It was dawn before she fell asleep.

The next day the plastic surgeon removed the stitches from Carole's face. She was adamant in her refusal to allow him to operate on her scar.

"I don't care how good he is. *He's* not going to touch me."

Dr. Citrin quietly left the room.

Lips set tightly, her mother spoke under her breath. "Don't be rude. We'll have to wait until the cut heals, anyway. There's time to do it before school starts. Carole, why live with a scar?"

"Mom, I'm not saying I'll never have the surgery. It's just out of the question right now." Carole shook her head. "I can't explain it."

"Are you at least willing to discuss this with your father?"

"Mother, the issue is closed."

Her mother did not reply. They drove home in silence.

On the kitchen table Amy had left a scribbled note: *A lady named Nicky called twice from Quebec. She's calling back. Mom, I went riding — home for dinner.*

In the den Carole lay down to await Nikki's call. When the phone rang she hopped to the bar and caught it on the second ring. After the first few words, Carole closed the den doors. They talked for an hour.

232

Journal Entry — July 16, 1973

Dear Nikki,

Sweet love, thank you for loving me — scar and all. Only you would be so totally accepting of me. I'm not sure why I want the damned thing. It's a trophy as well as a mark. I'm not willing to erase something so painfully earned.

I'm puzzled, by your not wanting me to tell my family about us. You called our love private. I see it as a secret, and secrets stem from shame — something I don't feel. I'm going to follow my intuition. If the time feels right, I'll tell.

This afternoon I'll find a lab where I can print my pictures. Actually, the silence of the darkroom will be paradise. I had forgotten what it's like living here in the middle of so much activity.

Mom's already scheduled shopping excursions and visits to relatives. This morning when she offered to host a gathering of my old friends, I nearly bashed her. Of course, Dad and Amy agreed with her. They try so hard to make me feel at home. I'm such a bitch. Part of it is our separation and knowing what everybody's going to do, what everybody's going to say. Another part is their assumptions about my feelings. Mom and Dad's favorite line is, "I understand."

Amy and I talked last night until late. I was right — she's having sex. With her riding instructor. That's her big secret. He's thirty-five. She asked about the men in my life. I told her about John. I kept my secret. If Mom and Dad only knew how their little princesses turned out.

Your next stop is Three Rivers. It made me laugh to hear you so upset about sharing the limelight with another strip. You're so vain, Nikki. I love it.

233

I purposefully didn't ask how you're going to get there or how you're going to move all that luggage without me. Yes, I know I'm helpless now, but I don't like the idea that you can navigate through life without me. I love knowing you need me, that my feelings are important to you. No, I'll never tire of you, my sweet, dearest love, my red-haired lady.

Journal Entry — July 21, 1973

Everything I suspected about myself is true. I've changed because of Nikki. I'm glad.

Last weekend Mom wheedled me into going shopping, and when we returned the house was full of my old girlfriends. I think it was embarrassing for all of us because we never stayed in touch, but none of them could say no to my mother — especially when she always remembers their birthdays.

The party was nice as long as we talked about the past. The present for them is boyfriends, jobs, school. A few have kids.

Their lives seem so predictable. I felt older — more worldly. What would they say if they knew I was a lesbian? Bored, I fantasized tapping my glass and announcing, "Did you guys know I'm . . ."

To think I once worried about not knowing what the future might bring and whether I'd be ready to handle the unexpected. What a fool I was. Now I welcome the unknown.

How understanding Nikki has been with me. Now that I'm here, surrounded by my family, I see that when I criticized her marriage to Bert, her dancing, I was imposing their values on her. I've got to get Mom and Dad out of my head.

The only one at the party who seemed interested in the world beyond here was Robbie, who's an anthro and has been living with the Kwakiutl Indians. She was fascinated to hear about the footage I shot in Coulterville and is coming over to see it when I finish. No mention of men in her life. I wonder.

The party showed me that I can't live here again. Easy as I have it at home, I live for my reunion with Nikki. Right now I'm ready to fly back to Canada or L.A.

I miss the freedom and the anonymity of L.A. Something about this visit reminds me of being locked up in my room in Quebec. I prefer a larger canvas for my life.

Journal Entry — July 23, 1973

Today was the first time I didn't hear from her. She's called every day since I've been here. In fact, Mom asked if my friend was in trouble because she keeps calling long distance.

The last time we talked she made me promise to trust her, no matter what. More times than usual she said she loved me. She asked several times if I loved her. I think I finally convinced her.

I can see why Mom's curious. The only thing I told my family about the summer was that I was photographing Indian life in Quebec and that some dancers were paying me to shoot their trip.

Journal Entry — August 2, 1973

I'm a wreck. I've been trying to reach Nikki all week. She hasn't called for ten days. I know something's happened. She's supposed to be in Montreal this week. They said she left after the fifth night. I traced her back to Athabaska and Three Rivers. She was on schedule there.

I don't have Bert's private number. Janice is supposed to call me after she talks to him. Goddamn you Nikki! Why are you doing this to me?

I haven't been able to eat or sleep. My parents are freaked to see me so upset. I can't help myself. I told Dad that my friend is missing and he thinks I should call the American Consulate. At first I thought he was being absurd. But now it doesn't sound like such a bad idea.

Journal Entry — August 5, 1973

Janice called only to tell me she'd call again when she had news. She told me not to worry, that Nikki knew how to take care of herself.

That bitch knows something and isn't telling me.

Well, it's all out now. Mom knows. She woke me this morning and asked about my frantic calls to L.A. and Quebec. Was I in some kind of trouble? Who was I calling? The entire household was upset because of me. I offered to leave for L.A. immediately. That only made things worse. She said pointblank, "What's going on between you and your friend?"

I hugged her. "Don't be mad. I love her," I said and told her how happy Nikki has made me this last year. That was that. I don't know why I was so uptight about telling.

I watched Mom's body — she didn't tense up or anything. I didn't appreciate her asking, "If she loves you so much, why hasn't she called? She must know you'd be frantic by now."

Going out the door she said, "I wish it were otherwise. It's against our religion. No one in our family has ever done this. Maybe it's something you'll work through. No need to let your father know about this yet."

I asked her to please be happy for me. She said, "Don't tell me what to feel. I'm not going to give you a hard time about this, but don't expect my blessing either."

Journal Entry — August 8, 1973

No news from her yet. I'm keeping busy. If I think about her, I'll go nuts. Every day when I come home I expect to hear that she's called. Things have sort of calmed down around here. Now that Mom knows, I'm less frantic. It's like I don't have to carry it all by myself anymore. Mom said the next move is up to Nikki. She knows where I am. What I'm really worried about is whether Nikki still wants me.

Robbie says my pictures of the Indians are great. The scenes of the women sitting around the radio laughing and talking capture their displacement. The kids' smiles show that they haven't caught on to the poverty that surrounds them.

This might very well be the best work I've ever done. I remember how angry Nikki was when that man threw us out of the housing project. And then we had that big fight. Seems funny now.

Robbie submitted my pictures to the University of Washington Native American Museum where she's doing her internship.

I made 18″ by 24″ pictures of Nikki getting ready for her road trip. It was wonderful. The bigger I made her, the more real she became. I have shots of her laughing, brooding, concentrating, and being angry with me and my camera. She's beautiful in every mood.

I showed them to my family and their perceptiveness surprised me. They saw beyond Nikki's beauty. Dad took his time looking through them. I watched him. He took in every curve and curl of her. Unbeckoned, he announced that his favorite was the shot where Nikki is looking pensively at a costume. She has that faraway look she can sometimes get, as if staring beyond an object to a mysterious somewhere. "I see a sadness in her that's got nothing to do with the costume."

Amy liked the one where Nikki is angry at the camera. She's sure Nikki has a temper. "I can tell," Amy insisted. I said Nikki explodes once in a great while. I didn't know what else to say. She's always been so calm with me, but then there's the time she picked up the pipe and smashed the guy who hit me.

Mom's reaction was best. She said Nikki was "a sensitive person hiding behind her beauty." When Amy called Nikki gorgeous, Mom agreed. She smiled, took my hand and squeezed it. I got a big lump in my throat.

God Nikki, please call.

My face and leg are healed. My scar looks great. School starts next month. Mom's right, I must move on with my life.

I'm reading too much into Nikki's silence, leaving myself to flounder in uncertainty. All that is keeping me

*from going insane is her last phone call when she made me
promise to trust her, no matter what.*

*I'm heading back to L.A. to search for her there. Mom's
giving me money in case I need it for phone calls or travel.
In turn I promised to start school in September, whether
Nikki shows up or not. I won't die without her, but the
pain would last forever.*

"Mom, I'd forgotten how good your brisket is," Carole
said. She reached for another helping. "I'll have to diet
when I get back to school."

The door chimes rang. Her father shoved a forkful
into his mouth and arose. A moment later he came into
the kitchen, eyes wide in surprise. "Carole, it's the girl in
the pictures!"

CHAPTER TWENTY-SIX

Nikki had never looked more beautiful. Her long hair shorn, she now wore a chic feathered hairstyle. In a Portland Travelodge overlooking the Willamette River, her nude body was stretched languorously across the rumpled bed. Carole lay next to her, relishing the end of loneliness, anxiety, uncertainty.

"You don't look so angry now," Nikki teased.

"But I had reason to be. Dad wasn't kidding when he said I'd been worried sick about you. That's why Mom asked about you and me."

"I thought we had decided not to tell your folks," Nikki chastised her.

"Don't worry," Carole said reassuringly. "Mom's the only one who knows. It's better that way. I could tell that Dad and Amy really liked you — they looked disappointed when I insisted we leave right after dinner. You took so long eating I could have killed you." Carole added, "Mom liked you too, in spite of herself."

"Thank God I didn't know she knew. I'd have been so nervous talking to them. I'm glad I didn't accept your Dad's invitation to stay at your house."

"How long do you plan to be here?" Carole asked, hesitantly.

Nikki caressed Carole's face. "How soon can you come home with me?"

"As soon as you convince me there was a reason for you not to call."

A look of sadness crossed Nikki's face. She shook her head as if to dispel an unpleasant memory. "It's a simple story, but parts of it are going to upset you. I'd just finished the midnight show in Montreal. Two officers came backstage and informed me that dancing bottomless was illegal there."

"I knew I shouldn't have left you." Carole buried her head between Nikki's breasts.

Nikki tousled Carole's hair and burst out laughing. "My love, what could you have done? It was no big deal. In fact it was the best thing that could have happened to me. When they took away my work permit, something snapped." She paused. "I cancelled the tour. Through

Janice I contacted Precious Pearl at the Crystal Palace. She jumped at the chance to take over my contract."

Tensing, Carole asked, "What did Bert say about all this?"

"He didn't care as long as my replacement had long legs and a good wardrobe, which is Pearl down to the last rhinestone. Club owners always want an out-of-town headliner." Nikki laughed. "What cold be more exotic than Precious Pearl, the former Miss Nude Tokyo? I flew Pearl to Quebec. That's the story, darling." Nikki reached over and took Carole into her arms.

Beneath the bravado of her lover's patter, Carole sensed there was more to the story. She pressed closer. "So why the two week silence?"

"I needed to be by myself. I flew to L.A. to talk to Bert and file for divorce. He argued that love was making me blind. He wouldn't discuss it until I thought things over for a week. I spent a long lonely week in my apartment." Nikki's voice deepened. "I was dying to call, but understand, I had to wrestle with this alone. And believe me, I never felt more alone. In the end I not only went through with the divorce, I quit working for him. I'm on my own. Happy?"

Carole checked her impulse to shout with joy. "Not if it's causing you pain."

"Choosing to live without Bert's support scares the hell out of me." Her voice rose. "I'll make it. I'm not sure how, but I'll do it. Janice said she could find an opening for me at the theatrical booking agency where she works. I'll suffer through that or something else for as long as it takes. I vowed that I'd finish school. I will."

"I believe in you," Carole said, then asked, "but are *you* sure?"

Tenderly, Nikki cupped Carole's chin. "I wasn't sure if it was the right decision. Then I saw your face again."

Carole, her mother, and Nikki sat in a booth in the airport lounge waiting for the morning flight to Los Angeles. Carole's mother had insisted that she be the one to drive them. Carole feared a confrontation. The rigidity of her mother's body intensified her fear.

As soon as the waitress placed three coffees in front of them, Carole's mother said, "Listen, what you do with your private lives is your choice — but it shouldn't hurt those who love you."

Carole wrinkled her nose in disapproval. "I hate the thought of shielding Dad. He's a tough guy. Mom, I see our love as something beautiful. And when you insist on protecting him, you're turning our love into something dirty."

Her mother clasped her hands tightly around the cup. "Let me assure you of a couple of things. If you two live together as you're intending to do, he'll figure it out himself, believe me. Yes, he's tough, but he's also vulnerable. He's used to being in control. This business is too far out for him. Maybe I'm just thinking about myself. When I can handle it better, I'll be able to handle his knowing about it, too."

Carole raised her voice. "I've never lied to Dad. I feel like I'm changing our entire relationship — like I'm not meeting him squarely."

Her mother laughed nervously. "You show up sick, out of nowhere. We take care of you. You want to drop a bomb on us and go off into the sunset with your girlfriend. Does that sound fair and square to you?"

243

"No, it doesn't," Nikki said, turning to Carole. "If your Dad could spend time with us and see how happy we are, the news would be easier for him."

"He saw how miserable I was when I didn't hear from you," Carole angrily reminded Nikki.

"Talk about wearing your heart on your sleeve," her mother remarked disapprovingly.

Nikki asked evenly, "Ladies, where is this conversation going? There isn't time to get emotional." To Carole's mother she said, "What do you want resolved?"

The woman shook her head. "I don't know. I'm so angry at both of you. You're leaving me alone with a time bomb. My husband will blame me for letting Carole return to L.A. without some kind of explanation — without some effort to change her mind. I'm sure he'll accuse me of mishandling this."

Carole reached over to her. "Mom, you're the one who told me not to tell Dad. If you want I'll fly back at winter break and talk to him. I'm more than willing to. I want to do it."

Her mother was unable to control her tears. "That may work." She dried her eyes. "I'm sorry, Carole dear, I don't want your memories of home to be unhappy. Nikki, please understand how I feel. It's not personal. I'm sure you're a fine lovely woman, why else would Carole love you so much?"

"I understand your pain Mrs. Wolston," Nikki said. "It was just as hard for my mom to accept this lifestyle."

"I'm sure you never saw the true pain you caused her. It hurts to know your daughter has chosen a way of life that society doesn't accept."

Gently, Nikki said, "Society has no business and no right to be in our bedroom."

* * * * *

The trade-off for enduring September's heat and smog
in L.A. is the year's most beautiful sunsets. Camera
raised, Carole recorded Nikki hand-feeding Gypsy, the
stray cat.

The past three weekends Carole and Nikki had gone
to Holmby Park so that Nikki could pursue her courting
of the cat.

She had taken him home the first weekend. Gypsy's
howling awakened the neighborhood and at dawn a
sleepy, apologetic Nikki returned him to what he
considered home.

Undaunted, she returned the following week armed
with sardines, kibble, milk and patience. Gypsy was
suspicious. As Nikki waited him out, Carole's camera
marked the stand-off.

The cat moved snake-like toward her. Head raised,
nostrils flared, he kept a wary eye on her, his tail a rigid
antenna poised to intercept any sudden movement.
Statue-like, Nikki sat on the picnic table with a can of
sardines. "Yes, my love," she whispered. "Come forward.
Trust me."

Gypsy stared at her with green-yellow eyes. Again he
widened his nose toward the aromatic can. Carole's
camera sounded with each movement.

He's a goner, Carole decided.

The cat lapped the oil from the top of the can, then
stepped back. Nikki reached into the can and pried out
some fillets. She crumbled them and offered them to the
stray. "Take this, Gypsy. Nothing will hurt you."

Gypsy waited for her to drop the pieces before
lowering his head. He ate, his eyes moving furtively
between the food and Nikki.

Nikki wiped her hands on a paper towel, leaving the food on the table. "That's all I want to do today. We'll come back next week."

She moved toward the car without looking back. Gypsy stared at her. She opened the car door and called him to her. Gypsy opted for the remaining scraps.

The following weekend Nikki did not go to Holmby Park. "I want him to miss me," she said to Carole.

When she returned, Gypsy looked at her as though she were a total stranger. "I see he's managed without me," grumbled Nikki. "The week I labored about my decision with Bert, I spent here with Gypsy. He was what mattered. I believe in his cat instincts — they're the same as mine."

She offered the cat center cuts of the sardines, laying them down and stepping away. Carole watched the cat stare unblinkingly at her, then at Nikki.

Air entered lungs and somewhere between nose, stomach and head, a connection took place. Gypsy moved toward the soft cooing woman. He accepted her open hand, caressed himself against her nails, his sleek muscular body drawing pleasure from her strong consistent hand, then he returned to the sardines and ate.

Carole's camera framed the scene.

She shot the next roll of Nikki and the cat two weeks later in their apartment, the cat curled comfortably on the lap of a drowsing Nikki.

A few of the publications of
THE NAIAD PRESS, INC.
P.O. Box 10543 ● Tallahassee, Florida 32302
Phone (904) 539-9322
Mail orders welcome. Please include 15% postage.

HIGH CONTRAST by Jessie Lattimore. 264 pp. Women of the
Crystal Palace.   ISBN 0-941483-17-7 $8.95

OCTOBER OBSESSION by Meredith More. Josie's rich, secret
Lesbian life.   ISBN 0-941483-18-5   8.95

LESBIAN CROSSROADS by Ruth Baetz. 276 pp. Contemporary
Lesbian lives.   ISBN 0-941483-21-5   9.95

BEFORE STONEWALL: THE MAKING OF A GAY AND
LESBIAN COMMUNITY by Andrea Weiss & Greta Schiller.
96 pp., 25 illus.   ISBN 0-941483-20-7   7.95

WE WALK THE BACK OF THE TIGER by Patricia A. Murphy.
192 pp. Romantic Lesbian novel/beginning women's movement.
                                       ISBN 0-941483-13-4   8.95

SUNDAY'S CHILD by Joyce Bright. 216 pp. Lesbian athletics, at
last the novel about sports.   ISBN 0-941483-12-6   8.95

OSTEN'S BAY by Zenobia N. Vole. 204 pp. Sizzling adventure
romance set on Bonaire.   ISBN 0-941483-15-0   8.95

LESSONS IN MURDER by Claire McNab. 216 pp. 1st in a stylish
mystery series.   ISBN 0-941483-14-2   8.95

YELLOWTHROAT by Penny Hayes. 240 pp. Margarita, bandit,
kidnaps Julia.   ISBN 0-941483-10-X   8.95

SAPPHISTRY: THE BOOK OF LESBIAN SEXUALITY by
Pat Califia. 3d edition, revised. 208 pp.   ISBN 0-941483-24-X   8.95

CHERISHED LOVE by Evelyn Kennedy. 192 pp. Erotic
Lesbian love story.   ISBN 0-941483-08-8   8.95

LAST SEPTEMBER by Helen R. Hull. 208 pp. Six stories & a
glorious novella.   ISBN 0-941483-09-6   8.95

THE SECRET IN THE BIRD by Camarin Grae. 312 pp. Striking,
psychological suspense novel.   ISBN 0-941483-05-3   8.95

TO THE LIGHTNING by Catherine Ennis. 208 pp. Romantic
Lesbian 'Robinson Crusoe' adventure.   ISBN 0-941483-06-1   8.95

THE OTHER SIDE OF VENUS by Shirley Verel. 224 pp.
Luminous, romantic love story.   ISBN 0-941483-07-X   8.95

DREAMS AND SWORDS by Katherine V. Forrest. 192 pp.
Romantic, erotic, imaginative stories.   ISBN 0-941483-03-7   8.95

MEMORY BOARD by Jane Rule. 336 pp. Memorable novel about an aging Lesbian couple.   ISBN 0-941483-02-9   8.95

THE ALWAYS ANONYMOUS BEAST by Lauren Wright Douglas. 224 pp. A Caitlin Reese mystery. First in a series.   ISBN 0-941483-04-5   8.95

SEARCHING FOR SPRING by Patricia A. Murphy. 224 pp. Novel about the recovery of love.   ISBN 0-941483-00-2   8.95

DUSTY'S QUEEN OF HEARTS DINER by Lee Lynch. 240 pp. Romantic blue-collar novel.   ISBN 0-941483-01-0   8.95

PARENTS MATTER by Ann Muller. 240 pp. Parents' relationships with Lesbian daughters and gay sons.   ISBN 0-930044-91-6   9.95

THE PEARLS by Shelley Smith. 176 pp. Passion and fun in the Caribbean sun.   ISBN 0-930044-93-2   7.95

MAGDALENA by Sarah Aldridge. 352 pp. Epic Lesbian novel set on three continents.   ISBN 0-930044-99-1   8.95

THE BLACK AND WHITE OF IT by Ann Allen Shockley. 144 pp. Short stories.   ISBN 0-930044-96-7   7.95

SAY JESUS AND COME TO ME by Ann Allen Shockley. 288 pp. Contemporary romance.   ISBN 0-930044-98-3   8.95

LOVING HER by Ann Allen Shockley. 192 pp. Romantic love story.   ISBN 0-930044-97-5   7.95

MURDER AT THE NIGHTWOOD BAR by Katherine V. Forrest. 240 pp. A Kate Delafield mystery. Second in a series.   ISBN 0-930044-92-4   8.95

ZOE'S BOOK by Gail Pass. 224 pp. Passionate, obsessive love story.   ISBN 0-930044-95-9   7.95

WINGED DANCER by Camarin Grae. 228 pp. Erotic Lesbian adventure story.   ISBN 0-930044-88-6   8.95

PAZ by Camarin Grae. 336 pp. Romantic Lesbian adventurer with the power to change the world.   ISBN 0-930044-89-4   8.95

SOUL SNATCHER by Camarin Grae. 224 pp. A puzzle, an adventure, a mystery — Lesbian romance.   ISBN 0-930044-90-8   8.95

THE LOVE OF GOOD WOMEN by Isabel Miller. 224 pp. Long-awaited new novel by the author of the beloved *Patience and Sarah*.   ISBN 0-930044-81-9   8.95

THE HOUSE AT PELHAM FALLS by Brenda Weathers. 240 pp. Suspenseful Lesbian ghost story.   ISBN 0-930044-79-7   7.95

HOME IN YOUR HANDS by Lee Lynch. 240 pp. More stories from the author of *Old Dyke Tales*.   ISBN 0-930044-80-0   7.95

EACH HAND A MAP by Anita Skeen. 112 pp. Real-life poems that touch us all.   ISBN 0-930044-82-7   6.95

SURPLUS by Sylvia Stevenson. 342 pp. A classic early Lesbian
novel.   ISBN 0-930044-78-9   6.95

PEMBROKE PARK by Michelle Martin. 256 pp. Derring-do
and daring romance in Regency England.   ISBN 0-930044-77-0   7.95

THE LONG TRAIL by Penny Hayes. 248 pp. Vivid adventures
of two women in love in the old west.   ISBN 0-930044-76-2   8.95

HORIZON OF THE HEART by Shelley Smith. 192 pp. Hot
romance in summertime New England.   ISBN 0-930044-75-4   7.95

AN EMERGENCE OF GREEN by Katherine V. Forrest. 288
pp. Powerful novel of sexual discovery.   ISBN 0-930044-69-X   8.95

THE LESBIAN PERIODICALS INDEX edited by Claire
Potter. 432 pp. Author & subject index.   ISBN 0-930044-74-6   29.95

DESERT OF THE HEART by Jane Rule. 224 pp. A classic;
basis for the movie *Desert Hearts.*   ISBN 0-930044-73-8   7.95

SPRING FORWARD/FALL BACK by Sheila Ortiz Taylor.
288 pp. Literary novel of timeless love.   ISBN 0-930044-70-3   7.95

FOR KEEPS by Elisabeth Nonas. 144 pp. Contemporary novel
about losing and finding love.   ISBN 0-930044-71-1   7.95

TORCHLIGHT TO VALHALLA by Gale Wilhelm. 128 pp.
Classic novel by a great Lesbian writer.   ISBN 0-930044-68-1   7.95

LESBIAN NUNS: BREAKING SILENCE edited by Rosemary
Curb and Nancy Manahan. 432 pp. Unprecedented autobiographies
of religious life.   ISBN 0-930044-62-2   9.95

THE SWASHBUCKLER by Lee Lynch. 288 pp. Colorful novel
set in Greenwich Village in the sixties.   ISBN 0-930044-66-5   8.95

MISFORTUNE'S FRIEND by Sarah Aldridge. 320 pp. Historical Lesbian novel set on two continents.   ISBN 0-930044-67-3   7.95

A STUDIO OF ONE'S OWN by Ann Stokes. Edited by
Dolores Klaich. 128 pp. Autobiography.   ISBN 0-930044-64-9   7.95

SEX VARIANT WOMEN IN LITERATURE by Jeannette
Howard Foster. 448 pp. Literary history.   ISBN 0-930044-65-7   8.95

A HOT-EYED MODERATE by Jane Rule. 252 pp. Hard-hitting
essays on gay life; writing; art.   ISBN 0-930044-57-6   7.95

INLAND PASSAGE AND OTHER STORIES by Jane Rule.
288 pp. Wide-ranging new collection.   ISBN 0-930044-56-8   7.95

WE TOO ARE DRIFTING by Gale Wilhelm. 128 pp. Timeless
Lesbian novel, a masterpiece.   ISBN 0-930044-61-4   6.95

AMATEUR CITY by Katherine V. Forrest. 224 pp. A Kate
Delafield mystery. First in a series.   ISBN 0-930044-55-X   7.95

THE SOPHIE HOROWITZ STORY by Sarah Schulman. 176
pp. Engaging novel of madcap intrigue.   ISBN 0-930044-54-1   7.95

THE BURNTON WIDOWS by Vickie P. McConnell. 272 pp. A
Nyla Wade mystery, second in the series.   ISBN 0-930044-52-5   7.95

OLD DYKE TALES by Lee Lynch. 224 pp. Extraordinary
stories of our diverse Lesbian lives.   ISBN 0-930044-51-7   7.95

DAUGHTERS OF A CORAL DAWN by Katherine V. Forrest.
240 pp. Novel set in a Lesbian new world.   ISBN 0-930044-50-9   7.95

THE PRICE OF SALT by Claire Morgan. 288 pp. A milestone
novel, a beloved classic.   ISBN 0-930044-49-5   8.95

AGAINST THE SEASON by Jane Rule. 224 pp. Luminous,
complex novel of interrelationships.   ISBN 0-930044-48-7   8.95

LOVERS IN THE PRESENT AFTERNOON by Kathleen
Fleming. 288 pp. A novel about recovery and growth.
   ISBN 0-930044-46-0   8.95

TOOTHPICK HOUSE by Lee Lynch. 264 pp. Love between
two Lesbians of different classes.   ISBN 0-930044-45-2   7.95

MADAME AURORA by Sarah Aldridge. 256 pp. Historical
novel featuring a charismatic "seer."   ISBN 0-930044-44-4   7.95

CURIOUS WINE by Katherine V. Forrest. 176 pp. Passionate
Lesbian love story, a best-seller.   ISBN 0-930044-43-6   8.95

BLACK LESBIAN IN WHITE AMERICA by Anita Cornwell.
141 pp. Stories, essays, autobiography.   ISBN 0-930044-41-X   7.50

CONTRACT WITH THE WORLD by Jane Rule. 340 pp.
Powerful, panoramic novel of gay life.   ISBN 0-930044-28-2   7.95

YANTRAS OF WOMANLOVE by Tee A. Corinne. 64 pp.
Photos by noted Lesbian photographer.   ISBN 0-930044-30-4   6.95

MRS. PORTER'S LETTER by Vicki P. McConnell. 224 pp.
The first Nyla Wade mystery.   ISBN 0-930044-29-0   7.95

TO THE CLEVELAND STATION by Carol Anne Douglas.
192 pp. Interracial Lesbian love story.   ISBN 0-930044-27-4   6.95

THE NESTING PLACE by Sarah Aldridge. 224 pp. A
three-woman triangle—love conquers all!   ISBN 0-930044-26-6   7.95

THIS IS NOT FOR YOU by Jane Rule. 284 pp. A letter to a
beloved is also an intricate novel.   ISBN 0-930044-25-8   8.95

FAULTLINE by Sheila Ortiz Taylor. 140 pp. Warm, funny,
literate story of a startling family.   ISBN 0-930044-24-X   6.95

THE LESBIAN IN LITERATURE by Barbara Grier. 3d ed.
Foreword by Maida Tilchen. 240 pp. Comprehensive bibliography.
Literary ratings; rare photos.   ISBN 0-930044-23-1   7.95

ANNA'S COUNTRY by Elizabeth Lang. 208 pp. A woman
finds her Lesbian identity.   ISBN 0-930044-19-3   6.95

PRISM by Valerie Taylor. 158 pp. A love affair between two
women in their sixties.   ISBN 0-930044-18-5   6.95